"Mum, do we have to have her?"

Wearily, Mary sat down with her mug of tea. "For the umpteenth time. Yes."

Beth sighed, kicking her legs over the arm of the armchair. "Purple nails and lipstick and pierced ears when she was ten! And bubble gum in her hair, where she hadn't shaved it half off."

Her mother's lips quirked at the memory of Beth's appalled meeting with her cousin Tanya two years before. "Maybe she's improved," she consoled.

"What, you mean she's changed into a handsome toad?"

Mary slapped her mug down on the top of the gas fire. "Oh, for goodness sake, Beth. You're fourteen - act it, instead of sulking like a child. I'm no happier than you are, but she's family, so we help her."

Beth squirmed. "But she'll be taking up a room. Can we afford it, mum?"

Her mother snorted. "No. That's why she won't be taking up a room."

"What?" Beth sat up suddenly. "You don't mean she's got to share with me? No! I won't have her prying into all my things, and leaving her mucky chewing gum everywhere!" She jumped up and marched for the door.

Despite her plumpness, Mary beat her to it.

"Now, listen to me, Beth! When I had the car crash and couldn't walk for a year, Liz took you in, even though she had a sickly new baby." Her round, gentle face was severe. "And now she's going into hospital, so we take Tanya. That's only fair. Right?"

In spite of her resentment, Beth had to nod. "I suppose so. Okay!" she snarled. "I'll share."

"Politely!" her mother warned her sternly.

"Politely." Beth sniffed. "Can I go now? To get ready for our visitor! My spare bed's not made up yet."

Mary smiled at her daughter. "I think it's this muggy weather that's making us all irritable, pet. Feels like a thunderstorm. We'll all feel better when it breaks. There's only two couples booked in for dinner tonight. So if you get the messages, I can see to them and you can have some time off."

Rapidly, Beth abandoned her sulks. "The whole afternoon and evening free? Great! Got the list? Bank - all this to go in? Not bad, eh? Melon, chicken bits... Electric bill - good - er - good grief! Er - see you, mum!" The bill was horrendous, and she knew her mother was worried about money. The guest house was usually empty from November to March; there was dry rot in one of the bathroom floors - at least one - and the insurance bill was rocketing. Mary spent most of the winter writing children's stories, trying to make ends meet.

✠

Beth was chatting to a friend on one of the supermarket checkouts when Iona peered past her, pointed with her head and rolled her eyes. Beth glanced round.

A skinny little figure at the next till was buying a box of chocolates. The hem of her long black coat drooped unevenly round black skintight ski pants tucked into tatty black boots. In this sticky heat, how could she stand that wide-brimmed black felt hat pulled down over her straggly black hair? The thin hands laying out coins had black-painted nails, bitten right down to the quick, and several heavy silver rings. And that stuffed-nose Lancashire accent! No, oh no, please...

Beth swiftly hurried for the door. But her long fair hair, curling like Alice in Wonderland's down her back, was a giveaway. Behind her came a raucous yell.

"Ey up! Beth! Is you, ain't it? It's me, Tanya. Didn't yer see us?"

Reluctantly, she turned to the awful vision which was perkily trotting after her. She sighed. Yes, it was her cousin. No free evening.

"Hello, Tanya."

The two stared at each other for a few seconds.

Beth's heart sank. Tanya couldn't be even smaller and skinnier, could she? She had four or five pierced earrings in each ear, and some of the holes were disgustingly red and crusted.

And what was that round her neck? A silver chain with an upside-down cross on it? Yuck! Iona was making faces behind Tanya's back. She'd never live this down!

Tanya's heart sank. Beth wasn't so much square, as cubic! All fair and fat and normal. All that platinum blonde hair, natural, of course, never dream of bleaching it, and nice white blouse, and nice grey skirt, and nice white sandals... Stuffy, stuck-up and squeaky clean! Oh, 'eck! She grinned, half rueful, half cheeky. "Didn't think you'd see us so soon, did yer?"

"No, not till next week. You look just the same." Worse luck!

"You ain't changed much neither." Worse luck!

"What are you doing here?" Beth pulled herself together. "I mean, is Auntie Liz all right?"

Tanya chortled, the rows of silver earrings glinting and jingling. "Off to Majorca for a week, 'fore she goes into hospital. Last chance for a spree, see?"

Beth nearly exploded. So she and her mother had to put up - and put up with - Tanya, to let Aunt Liz have a week's holiday! What would mum say?

To her surprise, her mum didn't seem bothered. "You're very welcome, Tanya. If you'd phoned to let me know you were coming, we could have met you at the station."

"Weren't our fault, Aunt Mary." Tanya's rings flashed defensively as she waved her hands animatedly. "Called yer four times, but the line were engaged. Every time." She sensed their disbelief, and started talking even faster, fishing in her black nylon sports bag. "Got a pressie for yer, Aunt Mary. Mam sent it wi' her love." It was a pound box of chocolates.

"But you bought that in..." Beth caught her mother's glare. Tanya was bright red with anger and embarrassment.

"Thank you, lass. It was a kind thought." Mary smiled. "Right, Beth, take Tanya up and settle her in. Make up the bed, and clear a space for her clothes."

Tanya lifted her tatty bag. "This is it, Aunt Mary. Don't need much. Just T-shirts an' that. Black, o' course. A Goff, see!"

"A Goff?" Beth demanded. "What's a Goff?"

"You taking the mickey?"

"A Goth, you mean, Tanya?" Mary chuckled. "Not with it, Beth!"

"S'right. Goff. G-O-T-H, Goff! All black an' mysterious, right? See me pixie boots?" She displayed them proudly, not seeming to care that the toes were scuffed and crumpled, and the heels chipped and skinned. "Cracking fancy buckles, eh? One on me hatband, too, see - real silver! Fell off a lorry, or I'd never have afforded 'em."

Mary stifled a sigh. "Well, go on both of you, I've dinners to make."

Resigned, Beth led Tanya out into the tiny back hall of Firthview House.

"That's the dining room door, with the front hall and stairs on the far side of it. The lounge is right above. Four bedrooms on that floor. We live up these back stairs." On the first floor, she pointed to the doors. "That's the lounge. Room 3, here, has its own bathroom. 4 and 5 are along there."

A narrow spiral twisted up to two attic bedrooms and a tiny bathroom. Tanya stared round Beth's room, panting. Yellow bedspread and teddies. Oh 'eck! No carpet even, just a rug on the floorboards. And a view of just about the end of the world. To her annoyance, fatso wasn't out of breath at all. She tried to be nice.

"Them gold curtains is right swanky. An' the way the roof slopes down like an Arab tent, full o' Eastern Promise! Black paint an' a purple carpet, an' it'd be magic!"

Black and purple! Yuck! Beth was quite happy with her sunny yellow and white.

"I'm glad you like it." Stiffly, she dumped sheets and pillowcases on the spare divan under the sloping ceiling opposite her own. "This is yours. How many drawers do you want?"

"One'll do us. Trying to get away from being owned by things."

"What?" Beth plumped down on her own bed, automatically leaning forwards to avoid the ceiling close above her head. "What do you mean?"

Grinning mischievously, Tanya threw herself flat on her back on her bed. Her black T-shirt was rotted away under the arm, and the smell of stale sweat was spreading through the room. "Things owns yer. Got to look after 'em, an' scared to lose 'em. Ain't got nowt, yer free. See?"

Beth stared. She'd never heard anybody say things like that before. Especially not somebody two years younger than she was. And in that irritating stuffed-up voice, sounding every 'th' as 'f', 'ing' as 'ink', and 'uh' like 'oo'. And swearing, and smelly. Yuck. Huffily she stood up. One drawer? Ridiculous!

"I'll clear these two drawers for you, while you make the bed." She opened her top drawer. Disturbing all her tidy arrangements...

Tanya didn't move.

"Come on, Tanya," Beth urged. "Get the bed made up, and we'll go down and give mum a hand."

"I ain't no slave."

"What? You mean - you want me to make up your bed for you?"

Lounging, Tanya shrugged. "Please yerself."

"But..." Beth was dumbfounded. "You'll be sleeping in it. You should help make it up."

Tanya chuckled, smug and superior.

Superior? Smelly, dirty, lazy, disgusting, foul-mouthed...upsetting everybody and swearing and expecting to be waited on hand and foot and then daring to sneer... Hot, sticky, headachey and feeling put-upon, Beth suddenly gave up the struggle with her temper. "Well, I'm not a slave either!" she snarled. "You want food? You help with the cooking! You want clean plates to eat off? You help wash and dry them! You want to stay here, you help!" As Tanya sat up, Beth slammed the pillow down onto the smaller girl's chest, knocking her flat again. "Or you can clear right out again and sleep on the beach and die of pneumonia! See if I care!"

She knew she'd lost her temper, but she didn't care. Her voice rose and rose until she was shouting, leaning over Tanya on the bed. "Now, get up, and get that bed made up, and take a shower. You're grey and you stink! Wash your filthy, nitty hair and hurry up!" Her head was just bursting.

Insulted and angry, Tanya shoved the pillow off. "Ain't niffy! Or nitty!"

"Yes, you are! Horrid! And this isn't a pigsty! Now get a move on! And stop swearing!"

"Swearin'? I don't swear!"

"Hah! Only every second word! It's not clever or brave or anything, it just shows you're stupid and bad-mannered, and don't know proper, interesting words, and - and your mum didn't bring you up properly!" Beth was quoting rather confusedly from her mother.

"You leave me mam out o' this!" Tanya bounced up off the bed, shrieking. "Ain't nowt wrong wi' mam! She's better'n yours!"

Screeching, Beth slapped her. Tanya clawed her back.

At the back of her mind, Beth couldn't believe this; she hadn't behaved like this since nursery school.

Then, suddenly Mary was hauling Beth off, slapping them both to stop the hysteria.

"What's all this about?" she hissed. "I had a family going to take Room 3, but when they heard your carry-on, they decided not to stay! And I don't blame them! But that's a lot of money you've just cost me!"

They all stared at each other in anger and dismay.

"Beth - who started this?"

The girls glowered in silence.

"Tanya?"

"She said I stink."

"Well, she does!"

As Mary's face grew even sterner, Beth tried to excuse herself. It wasn't her fault!

"She won't help at all, not even by making her bed! She expects us to be her slaves!"

Mary drew a deep breath to calm herself. "Is that true, Tanya?" she asked. "Do you really want to stay here, in our house, and do nothing to help?"

Tanya was sniffing sulkily, head hanging, her lank hair hiding her face. "Didn't ask to come."

"We didn't ask to have you!"

"Quiet, Beth!" Mary checked her daughter's temper. After a pause, she continued, "Well, I think this is due to the close weather. Everybody's irritable. But I can't and I won't put up with fighting!" She looked at Tanya's unyielding face, and sighed, then frowned at her daughter.

"Beth, go and have a shower. Then Tanya can have one, and put on clean clothes, and we'll get those ones washed. She's been travelling in them since yesterday in this sticky heat, it's only natural she's been sweating. You'd be the same." Her tone firmed. "Let's not have anything like this again. Okay?"

She paused halfway down the stairs, to listen. Silence upstairs, thank goodness. There was a car drawing up outside. She pulled herself together and hurried on down.

The girls glared like fighting cats.

Beth turned away first, rubbing her scratched wrist. She felt ashamed of herself, and even more angry because of it.

Rubbing her red cheek, Tanya grumbled. "Bullyin'..." Luckily, the last word was lost.

"I'm not! You're just a disgrace! You're dirty and rude and selfish!" But mum had said to stop this. And there was that box of chocolates, which Tanya must have bought with her own money...

"Oh. Let's just get on!" Annoyed and confused, Beth bent to pick up her T-shirts that had been scattered all over the floor, to fold them and put them away tidily.

Tanya stood still, making no move towards

the bundle of sheets.

"What's wrong? Didn't your marvellous mum teach you how to make a bed?" Beth sneered.

"Course she did!" Tanya's voice was muffled.

Beth's lips tightened again. "Well, get a move on, then!" She shoved at Tanya's shoulder.

The smaller girl whipped round. "Don't touch us, you fat cow!" she screeched. "Or I'll curse yer!"

"I'm not fat!" Beth snarled. "You're just skinny! Curse me? Don't be daft!"

"Oh yes I will! An' my curses work! I'll curse yer to death!"

As Beth glowered, Tanya jumped up onto her bed, flinging her hands up as if to claw at the sky. Her knuckles cracked hard on the sloping ceiling above her. "Ow!" She collapsed, curling round her sore hands like a monkey with a bag of peanuts. Beth couldn't help it; she started to laugh.

Directly down the stairs from their room, Mary was showing a gentleman Room 4. She felt somehow nervous with this one and his cut-glass English voice. He looked around, stroking his moustache rather disdainfully.

"No, thank you. I definitely want to have private facilities."

Mary hid a sigh. If only she could afford to install private bathrooms for all the rooms. Then Tanya's shrieks echoed down the stairs. Mary's lips tightened. Again!

To her surprise, the gentleman was listening

with interest. "Who's the lively youngster?"

"Lively? Hmm. That's one way to put it!" Mary snorted. "My niece. Here for a holiday. Just arrived, and moving in to share with my daughter -"

"Ah, I see! Birds in their little nests agree, eh?" he chuckled. "Well, now, Mrs - er - Mackenzie, isn't it? Have you any rooms with their own facilities?"

"Just Room 3, here. But it's a big family room, and more expensive."

"That's all right. Can I see it? I'll pay the full family rate if it suits me."

Mary controlled a grin of delight.

"Charming! And the bathroom - I see. Yes, this will suit me very well."

His eyes were almost violet. Mary dragged her own gaze away from them with some effort. "That's fine. Would you like to come down and sign the register?"

At the desk in the front hall, the man took out a solid gold pen. "James Mandrake, Chelsea, London."

There was a sudden flash of lightning; thunder roared round the house. Mary jumped.

Mr Mandrake laughed pleasantly. "How very theatrical! Just like the appearance of a demon king in a pantomime!" he joked. "Only natural, of course, with a sorcerer's name like mine! May I have dinner here tonight, Mrs Mackenzie? Excellent. I'll get my cases. No, no, you stay in here."

His car was a gorgeously impressive, gold Porsche convertible. Mary closed the register. Full family rate, for just one person? Wonderful.

Mr Mandrake came back in with two cases, not hurrying in spite of the pouring rain. "I'll see you at dinner, then."

Mary wondered what material his suit was cut from. It hadn't looked wet at all... Would the chicken stretch to another one? Yes, just. And more potatoes...

Chapter 2

Upstairs, Beth couldn't help chuckling.

"What you sniggering at, fatso?" Tanya was sniffing, nursing her hands miserably.

"What's wrong, skin-and-bones? Broken a finger? Serve you right!"

"I'm okay. Let us alone!" Tanya snarled.

Beth sniffed disagreeably. But maybe Tanya didn't know how to put the cover on a duvet. It was tricky, if you hadn't had as much practice as Beth, and Tanya was much smaller. Or maybe she just had blankets at home. Beth's conscience niggled.

"Here, I'll do it - this time! You put on the pillowcases. I suppose you can do that much? And then I must get a shower, like mum said." She couldn't help herself. "I'm nearly as stinky as you."

Under the pillow she was struggling with, Tanya's voice was muffled with pillow and temper. "What's with the 'nearly'?"

"What? What did you -?" Beth's snarl was interrupted. A flash of lightning filled the whole room. Instantly, Beth was diverted. "Wow! Look at that!" A deep rolling boom of thunder shook the windows, and the cooling rain at last started to sheet down.

Tanya dropped the pillow to kneel on the window seat and lean out. "Ey, that's magic! Right on top of us, too! Fair tipping it down, eh?

Just smell the ozone!"

Beth sniffed, caught a ripe whiff of Tanya, and drew back. She tried to cover up. "I think it's the sea. I'd better shut the window before the rain soaks the cushion."

Tanya had noticed. Snooty madam! Her eyes glinted. "Don't want a wet bum next time yer sits there, eh? Yer mam might think you'd had a nasty accident!"

Stiffening angrily, Beth finished the bed in silence.

Somebody had to say something... "What's wrong with your mum anyway?"

Tanya shrugged one shoulder. "Cancer. Had a pain for months, but she wouldn't do nowt. Scared, see? Till she couldn't get up one morning. An' I called the doc, an' he said they'd take her in soon as they found her a bed. So mam phoned Aunt Mary. I said I could look after meself, an' visit her, I told her, but she said no. If the Social found us, they'd put us in a Home, an' she'd not risk that. Had to get us settled, she said. I didn't want to come here."

She wasn't the only one... Beth was surprised to find herself feeling sorry for her cousin but she couldn't say so, of course. "Couldn't you have stayed with a neighbour?"

Tanya snorted. "Round our block? You must be joking! It's not what you'd call a neighbourly neighbourhood. Things are so bleak at 'ome that even our Gran ran off to Texas wi' her new man to get away from it all. She wed again at near sixty. Ain't decent!"

Beth had to laugh at Tanya's outrage. Life looked like being more lively, anyway - if she could get the scraggy little scruff to clean up. If? She'd start right away. "Come on, get fresh clothes and let's clean up, then you can go out and look round the town. You can change in here." She noticed Tanya's hesitation. "What's wrong?"

"In front of you?" Tanya was defensive.

"Why not? We all get dressed together at the Academy, after games." And if Tanya's mother was really so ill, she might be here for a long time - worse luck, so she might as well get used to it.

The very same thoughts were going through Tanya's mind, but she was too proud to say it. Her voice was shrill with defiance. "Okay. Don't suppose it matters."

Tanya didn't have any socks. To Beth's horror, all Tanya had in her bag was a book on vampires, two more T-shirts - also rotten under the arms, and not very clean - and a huge baggy black jumper with soup stains and scorch marks down the front. Inside her boots, her feet were bare.

Beth bit her lip. "Tanya - er - look, would you like some more things? Guests have a habit of leaving things behind."

She wondered if Tanya would be offended,

18

but her cousin seemed quite happy at the idea. There weren't any socks small enough. She condescended to accept a pair of smallish red leggings - "Ain't black!" she complained - but dismissed with disdain two light T-shirts. Then she seized a man's shirt in bright purple. "Great!"

Beth sniffed. She could understand why it had been left more easily than why it had ever been bought in the first place. It would be a tent on Tanya - but at least it was clean. Boots and no socks - oh, yuck!

That afternoon, after Beth hurled all her clothes in the washing machine, Tanya went out for a walk. The sleeves of the huge purple shirt were rolled up to her elbows, and its hem hung knee-length over her red legs rising like sticks of rhubarb from her boots. Beth hoped nobody realised she came from Firthview...

Tanya made her feelings about Nairn perfectly clear. "Dead-end hole!"

Beth seethed, but held her tongue. Must be polite to the guest!

That evening, Tanya didn't appreciate the smooth organisation of the meal. "Do it right, and it's easy enough. Time and motion, that's all," Beth was showing off. "But if something goes wrong it can get a bit dramatic. Remember when we found the fish had gone bad, just half an hour before dinner, mum?"

"Don't I just!" Putting the dishcloths in to soak, Mary sank down with a sigh and a cup of tea. "Never mind, we coped. That's the main thing. As long as you keep your head, you're alright."

Tanya looked round the kitchen. "What do we do now, then? You ain't got no telly."

Beth sneered. "Sure. We're deprived!"

Mary laughed. "Do you play backgammon, Tanya?"

"What's that? Like Nintendo?"

Beth rolled her eyes.

Next morning Tanya slept on, while Beth got up at seven as usual.

"Hi!" Mary greeted her cheerfully. "Everybody's at eight except Mr Mandrake, he's at nine. How are you getting on with Tanya now?"

"Oh, we'll survive I suppose." Starting on her share of the breakfast work, Beth bit her lip. "Mum, she didn't come up by train." She eyed her mother sideways. "Aunt Liz didn't go to Majorca. When Tanya got back from school - she's only been going about two days a week, she says, for the last three years! - " She was horrified, but Mary just shook her head sadly. " - Aunt Liz just wasn't there. So Tanya waited two days, till she ran out of cash for food, and then she raided the electric meter. But she'd done it so often, there wasn't enough in it for a ticket, she says. I don't know how much to believe."

"Most of it, I'm afraid. I wonder where Liz is? Irresponsible, she is. Oh, well. So how did Tanya get here?"

"She hitched."

"Hitch-hiked? She must have been mad!"

"You mean you approve?" Beth was astonished.

"Don't be daft!" Mary snorted. "Of course I don't approve! It's dangerous! But at least she got here. No point now in telling her she shouldn't have. Take the milk jugs through, love. A right wee toughie, that one. Dauntless. Face up to anything... she may need to."

Beth grimaced. "You think Auntie Liz might be very ill?"

Her mother shrugged. "Could be. Tanya may need all her courage yet."

"All that silver junk," Beth muttered resentfully. "You know she pierced her ears herself with a needle and a cork behind! Did you see the scabs? And the skull rings? And that cross! Yuck!"

Mary laughed. "Oh, dear! Where did I get such a conventional daughter? Tastes differ, pet. That's everything in the warmer. Is the urn boiling? Okay. Stand by to repel boarders."

An hour later, Tanya wandered in, yawning and resplendent in purple shirt, rings, earrings and pendant, black lipstick, nail varnish and eyeliner. Her hair was shiny, though, and her neck was white. The first time in weeks, probably, Beth thought in grim satisfaction.

With the rush over, Mary had time to greet her with a smile. "Morning, pet! Sleep well?" She was pink and warm, washing dishes while Beth brought more through from the dining room.

"Yeah, fine, Aunt Mary." Tanya pinched half a sausage off a plate. Beth felt ill. She'd take any left in the warming dish, but to eat leftovers! Yuck!

"We'll be done here in another half-hour," Mary said. "Eight for dinner, and nobody leaving. A nice easy day. You girls can go for a picnic once the rooms are done." It might bring some colour into Tanya's white face. "Listen, there's Mr Mandrake coming down the stairs."

Neat in grey school skirt and white blouse, Beth served Mr Mandrake's coffee and toast, but as she dished up his meal, she dropped a tomato. "Oh, rats and botheration, look at that! It's splashed all down my front!"

"Rinse it right away, love, or we'll never clean it off."

Beth glanced at Tanya. Well, she was clean and decent. "Tanya, will you take Mr Mandrake's breakfast through?"

Tanya hesitated, feeling shy. But Aunt Mary was up to her elbows in dishes, and Beth was scrubbing at her blouse. She picked up the plate and went into the dining room.

The man sitting alone was big and broad all

22

over, even his face, and his wavy golden hair was longish. A right snazzy sweater. He had style, for an old geezer of about fifty. His eyes were dazzlingly blue as he sat back, smiling, to let her lay down the plate. "Thank-you. You're the cousin, aren't you? You don't look like Beth." Tanya stiffened, but he seemed to be approving. "Are you going to run a hotel when you grow up?"

She grinned. "No way! Gonna be a witch."

"Indeed? An unusual ambition. Do you know anything about it yet?"

She was pleased that he hadn't laughed, which was what she was used to. "Yeah. Read a pile o' books about it. An' I got a friend in Oldham who's into it."

"Ever tried casting a spell?" He seemed friendly. Too friendly perhaps. His eyes were bright blue. "Wasn't it you who I heard threatening to curse somebody?"

She blushed and turned aside, to avoid his eyes. "D'yer want owt else?" she asked coldly. None of his business what she'd said.

"I beg your pardon if I've offended you," he smiled. "I actually run an occult group in London. If you like, I could suggest books to read, and so on."

She was pleased in spite of her odd uneasiness with him. "Ta, be blooming magic!"

"What else?"

They both laughed. She relaxed, until he took hold of the upside-down cross dangling at her neck.

"You're an unusual girl, my dear. What's your name?"

"Tanya." She felt dizzy somehow, blinked and tugged away. As the cross slipped from his fingers, her head cleared.

"Right, Tanya. I'm delighted to have met you. Tell your aunt I'll certainly be staying another few days." He went on with his meal, smiling gently.

Tanya went back to the kitchen. There was something funny about him.

It had been taken for granted, now that she'd started, that Tanya would help with the housework. She considered arguing, but seeing a sneer ready to creep onto Beth's face, thought better of it.

Beth gave a flashy demonstration of how to change towels, clean a washbasin, polish the taps, mirror and glass, make up three beds perfectly, dust and vacuum a room, all in under fifteen minutes. Taking a deep breath, Tanya tried to copy her. It was hard work, though!

Beth nodded as they carried the vacuum cleaner down from the lounge. "You're getting the hang of it. All done, and it's not eleven yet." Yes, she should say it. "Thanks."

"No fuss," Tanya smirked. But she could do with a sit-down.

"We'll get the second lot of towels hung up and the sheets into the machine."

"Ain't we finished yet?"

In her turn, Beth smirked. "Just about. Not much to do this morning. Nobody leaving, no beds to change." Feeble little titch! Never done a hand's turn in her lazy life, probably. "And then we can get away. For the picnic, remember? If you fancy it?"

Picnics were for yokels. Oh, well. "Better than hanging about."

What wild enthusiasm! Beth's fists clenched for a second as they came into the kitchen. Oh, well. "We'll go to the old quarry at Kingsteps, mum, and we can get you some wild raspberries."

"Good idea, love. It's beautiful and sort of spooky - Tanya, you'll like it. And it's only a mile."

Tanya winced. A mile? To walk?

"I've made sandwiches," Mary said, hiding her smile at Tanya's expression. "Egg and pickle. Okay?"

"Sandwiches is butties at home in Oldham. Or tram-stoppers."

"Tram-stoppers? Good one! You must teach me more of your Lancashire words, Tanya."

"The Lanky twang, Aunt Mary."

"Oh, yes? Twang a bottle of coke out of the pantry!" Mary told Tanya, laughing. "All set, Beth? Have a good time."

As they went out, Mary breathed a sigh of

relief. They seemed to be getting on better now, thank goodness!

Tanya soon started to limp and hang behind. "How much further?"

"Stop grumbling, we're nearly there." Beth turned down a track, and then led Tanya over a chained gate and a barbed-wire fence.

"Hang on, me leggings is caught up!" Tanya was peeved. "An' me feet's killing me!" Beth didn't care, of course.

"Oh, I'm so sorry!" Beth sneered. Softy! "We're there." She pushed through some brambles and bushes.

Tanya's thin face was tight with annoyance as she limped after Beth. Better be worth it! Then she stopped and stared.

A ten-foot cliff shaded small elder trees leaning over to touch an oval of brown water. She gazed round, entranced in spite of herself. "Crikey!" She flopped down on the sunny shelf of flat rocks by the pool, kicking off her boots to splash her heels and white, crumpled toes, rubbed red and sore, pearled with blisters. "Ooh, cool! Magic! Fancy a dip?"

"We can't." Beth sat down beside her, dangling her feet over the edge. She plopped a stone into the water. "There were old cars dumped in the quarry hole, years ago. You can't swim at all, it's far too dangerous." She sighed. "They're going to fill it in next month. There's a couple of planes underneath, from the war. The local boys used to go diving for souvenirs out of them. Mum's got a magnet for her pins, that came out of one. That's what dad said, anyway."

"Did he get it himself?"

Beth grinned. "He never said, but I think so. He used to say that rules are made for a reason, and are meant to be obeyed, but then he'd sort of grin sideways and add, 'Usually'."

Tanya glanced over with resentful sympathy. "Miss him, don't yer?"

"M'hm." Lying back, Beth pointed south. "We had a farm, over that way. It was good there. But when he died, mum sold up, and we got the guesthouse." Yes, she missed him...

Tanya nodded. "Don't remember mine much."

Side by side, they sprawled back by the pool, basking in the sun. Lulled by the heat, the calm, the birdsong, Beth relaxed, falling gently asleep.

Tanya wasn't used to peace and quiet. When her feet were cool and the pain had faded, she soon grew bored. She sat up and fanned herself with her hat. "What about them raspberries?"

"What, already?" Reluctantly, Beth pushed herself to sit up. "You really don't like the country, do you, Tanya?"

"Huh! Messy. Nettles. An' spiders. Town for us, every time!"

The girls managed to gather about a pound of tiny, sweet raspberries. To Beth's annoyance, Tanya ate nearly as many as she put in the plastic bag. Then she bolted her sandwiches and fidgeted until they headed back.

Beth marched ahead. Her favourite place was spoiled now. She knew it was going to be destroyed anyway, but even the memory wouldn't be the same now - and it was all Tanya's fault!

Chapter 3

They'd scarcely gone a hundred yards when a big gold car drew up beside them. "Hello!" Smiling, Mr Mandrake looked at them. "Want a lift, girls?"

Tanya was already reaching gratefully for the door handle. "'ello, it's Mr Mandrake come to save our blisters!"

Beth was keen, too. She'd always wanted to ride in an open-top. "Thanks. It's very good of you." She climbed into the small back seat. As the car accelerated away, she sank back into the suede cushions, her hair blowing wildly. Oh, luxury!

In the front, Mr Mandrake was talking to Tanya. "What do you think of Nairn?"

She sniffed. "Smallsville. I bet nowt ever happens here!"

Mr Mandrake smiled. "Well, something has. You've come! And so have I!" They laughed together. He grew serious. "Maybe you can help me, you and Beth. I'm here on a kind of quest."

"Oh, yeah? What's that, then?" Tanya was interested. In the back, Beth sat forwards.

Mr Mandrake spoke gently. "Don't laugh, but I told you, Tanya, that I ran a magic circle in London? Well, last week, during a - a ceremony - I had a feeling that I must come north. I pay attention to such things. I was led here. Somewhere here there is something of importance, some item of magical significance, waiting for me to find it. I've been to the museum and the local newspaper, and they can't help me. Maybe you can suggest somebody else who could."

Beth was rather put off by the idea of magic ceremonies, but Tanya was enthralled.

"Not sure meself, but Beth might. All I know is... here, maybe that's it!"

"What?" he asked eagerly. Anything might be the clue...

"You ever heard o' the Brahan Seer?"

Of course he had! One of the most famous prophets of Britain. "Kenneth Odhar. Seventeenth century, wasn't it? Just on the other side of the Moray Firth. He had a scrying stone, a magical stone with a hole in it, and when he looked through it he saw -"

"Visions!" Tanya crowed. "Far-off, into the future an' that! Well, he were our ancestor! Kenneth Mackenzie!"

His excitement sank. "I'm sorry, Tanya. He can't have been. He had no children."

"I know that!" she almost yelled. "But his sister had a son! Me dad used to tell me about it. When Kenneth put his foot in it wi' the Countess o' Seaforth -"

"Silly idiot!" Beth commented, leaning forwards on the back of the front seats to talk to them. "Telling her in front of her friends that her husband was in Paris with another woman!"

"Give him his due, he tried to keep quiet!"

Tanya reminded her. "But she would have it, an' then she had him burned for it - but he threw the stone away -"

"And where it fell, a spring opened up and made a loch, and the stone was lost." Mr Mandrake carried on the tale, while he turned the car down towards the house. "He prophesied that a man with six fingers on each hand, and two navels, would find it."

"Right," Tanya nodded. "His sister's son's, son. An' dad said as we was descended from him. The family tried to use the stone for seeing, but they wasn't as good as old Kenneth - or maybe they just kept it quiet. They didn't want to get burned as well!"

"They used it for healing, too," Beth chipped in. "Dip it in holy water, dad said, say the right charm, and it'd heal cows, and babies with croup, and so on."

"What's croup?" Tanya asked.

"A choking cough." Mr Mandrake's voice was rather abstracted. Was this what he had been called here for? Yes - his skin was tingling. Sternly, he controlled his excitement. He mustn't scare the girls, not while they were friendly and helpful. "Here we are." He put on the brake. "So, where is the stone now?" He almost held his breath.

"Dunno." Tanya looked crestfallen. "Dad never said. It's disappeared."

"I'm afraid so," Beth confirmed. "I've no idea what happened to it. But I don't believe it, anyway. It's just a story. Not possible. Not really." She saw something in Tanya's face. "What is it, Tanya?" she challenged her cousin. "Do you believe in it?"

"Well…" Tanya spoke reluctantly. She'd better not tell everything she'd seen - not to a normal person like Beth. But a couple of the small things… "Cat, me pal in Oldham, she can see auras. A sort o' mental light all round yer. It changes depending on how yer feel. Can tell what mood yer in before she gets near yer. Or even if she's miles away - phoned us once to cheer us up, knew I were down in the dumps. Just knew. An' she often knows when something bad's going to happen - car crashes an' that. So I ain't so sure what's possible an' what ain't."

Beth sniffed and reached for the door handle. Mr Mandrake smiled. Now he understood why he had felt a tingle, an itch, a draw like a magnet pulling him out of London, to drive north and further northwards, seeking - he knew not what. It had drawn him to this town, to this particular house.

His own magic circle of witches in London was becoming dull. The slavish obedience he demanded from his disciples no longer satisfied him. There was nothing to excite and interest him, he was growing bored, ready for something new. This, at last, looked promising. To his surprise, he realised that the prickle of power that he was feeling came not just from the thought of the stone, the scrying stone, but also from the girls, especially from Tanya. The stone was valuable, he knew, and he was near, so near. He'd have it... and maybe the girls, too.

Beth gave Mr Mandrake the names of some local historians.

"I'll look them up. Come up and see me for a few minutes before dinner, and I'll tell you what I've discovered," he said. "And by then you'll maybe have thought of something else."

"Maybe mum knows?" Beth suggested. "Dad may have said something."

"Maybe. You know, this stone could be worth quite a lot if you could find it."

Suddenly, Beth perked up. "Enough to get the dry rot fixed? Put in new bathrooms?"

He laughed. "Almost certainly. Maybe you'd better not tell your mother why you're asking? It might get her hopes up too high." He smiled, his eyes bright blue and cheerful.

Tanya frowned. Why keep it quiet? But it wasn't important; and true enough, it would be a nice surprise for Aunt Mary.

Mary was glad to stop doing the accounts to have a cup of tea. After they'd handed over the raspberries, and put plasters on Tanya's blisters, and let her change back into her black jeans - to everybody's relief - Beth and Tanya exchanged glances.

"Er, mum." Beth cleared her throat. "You know dad used to tell stories about a magic stone?"

"You mean Kenneth Brown's scrying stone?" To her pleasure, Mary took the question casually. "Yes, sure, love."

"Was it true? How did it work?"

Mary shrugged. "Like a crystal ball, I suppose. He made a lot of prophecies, and some of them have apparently come true."

"Honest?" Tanya hadn't expected her so-ordinary aunt to know anything about this.

"Oh, yes. There was one about fire and water running through the streets of Inverness. They say that's the water and gas pipes - or electricity, I suppose. And he described ships sailing round the back of Tomnahurich Hill long before the canal was dreamed of. There was one about a well at Culloden running blood for three days. That's supposed to have been the battle of Culloden, in 1746. And then there was the big one about the fate of the Seaforths, when Lady Seaforth was going to burn him. That the line would die out, with the last Earl seeing his sons die before him, and the land going to a white-hooded lassie from the east who would kill her sister. That came true all right."

"Never!" Tanya exchanged a thrilled glance with Beth.

"Oh, yes. The heiress was the young widow of an Admiral Hood. In those days, a widow wore a white bonnet or hood, too. Well, one day she was driving her sister in a carriage when the horse bolted, and they crashed. Her sister died. So in a way she did kill her."

"You believe in it, then, mum?"

Mary shrugged. "Could be, love. Mind you, a lot of other people's sayings have got mixed in with his, I think. And he spoke in old Gaelic, that doesn't translate well into modern English, and figuratively at that - like that fire and water business; who's to know just what he meant? The prophecies weren't written down for years after he died, so anything could be added to the stories about him and who could argue? But it does seem there was something there."

Tanya was nearly bursting, trying not to grin in triumph. "Do you know what happened to the stone then, Aunt Mary?" she asked.

"Yes, has it come down the family to us?" Beth's face was eager.

Slowly, Mary shook her head. "I can't say. Sorry!" She chuckled at their disappointment. "Maybe it'll turn up some day soon!"

"I hope so!" Beth sighed.

Tanya nodded, but she felt an odd uneasiness.

That afternoon, when they heard Mr Mandrake come in, the girls ran up the stairs and tapped gently at the door of Room 3. When he answered and beckoned them in, Tanya had to dismiss a chill of unease, though it was to her that the broad, golden man smiled warmly. "Come in, come in! Did your mother know anything, Beth? No? Well, nobody else did either. But I've had an idea that may help."

The girls were puzzled.

"I told you that I knew about witchcraft, remember, Tanya? Well, that's because I am -" He paused. Take it easy, don't scare them off. "Well, let's say I have certain unusual skills."

Tantalising them, he slowly opened a small case lying on one of the spare beds. It was like a picnic case, fitted with straps to hold not plates, but odd-shaped bags and bundles, wrapped in glowing silks and velvets, mysterious and intriguing. Beth's fingers itched to investigate. These things were beautiful.

Tanya nibbled at her lip, worried by the shine in her cousin's eyes. She knew what this was all about. All those bags, like Cat's back in Oldham but much posher. Magic. Real magic. Dangerous, this was, if you didn't know what you were doing. Or if you did...

It was at her, not at Beth, that Mr Mandrake was looking. He had taken out a tiny light-blue bag with a silver draw cord. "You know, the only reason I stayed here was that I heard you, Tanya. You were threatening to curse your cousin. Weren't you? And I knew that you meant it."

"In a temper," Tanya protested. She tried to pass it off as a joke. "I swear terrible, Beth says, but -"

"No, no." He wasn't to be put off. "You've cursed somebody before. And it worked. You told me you wanted to be a witch. You do, don't you? You've felt the power in yourself." His eyes were blue and piercing.

She gave up, shrugging, to avoid a flat opposition to the mental pressure. "Done it once... A bully, see, roughing up a mate o' mine till he didn't know up from down. I ill-wished her, an' she were hit by a lorry same day, right outside the school gate. But I dunno - could've been just her bad luck." She didn't like the way Beth was staring at her, looking rather afraid.

He shook his head again. "No. It was you, I'm sure. I knew you had something. You see, I have power, too." He smiled at Beth. "Don't be alarmed, now. You have it as well. Everybody has. Everybody can sing, but some better than others. In the same way, everybody has power - mental, magic, whatever you call it. But most people have only a little, never notice it and can't use it. Tanya here has a great deal. On your own, Tanya, you've learned, somehow, how to - well, how to wave a mental fist about, as you might say, in a disorganised, inefficient, dangerous way. If you ignore your power, don't master it, or run away from it in fear and try to smother it, it may burst out some day in doing something dreadful. But with help - with my help - you can learn to control and use it. Like an Olympic athlete, Beth! Tanya can have that terrific thrill of glory, if she's not too scared."

His tone was a challenge, and even though she realised it, Tanya fired up. "Ain't scared o' nowt!" It wasn't true. She'd once seen Cat, days after a spell went wrong, still trembling and twitching. This was an awesome thing. Anybody who wasn't frightened was an idiot.

Mr Mandrake smiled. "Come and try this, then. It's quite harmless, I assure you." He was holding up a slender, delicately faceted point of milky crystal, about three centimetres long, hanging on a fine silver chain.

"Oh, that's pretty," Beth whispered.

He held it out to her. "Here." Smiling in pleasure, she held it up to twinkle in the light. "It's a pendulum, for dowsing. You've heard of that? Lots of people do it, to find water, and other things. Gold and treasure. Old drains, even. Most dowsers do it with wires or hazel twigs, on the ground, but it's quite possible on a map, too." While he spoke he was taking a map of the north of Scotland from the side table and flattening it out on the double bed. "I'm not very good at it, myself. But Tanya might be. Or you."

Beth hastily returned the crystal to him. "No, thanks."

Mr Mandrake didn't argue. He beckoned them to sit with him on the edge of the bed. "You see this, Tanya? There's the Moray Firth, and Inverness down in the corner. There's Chanonry Point, where Kenneth Odhar was burned, on the north side. Here's Nairn, where we are. You understand the map? Well, this is how you do it. Or how I do it, anyway. I think hard about what I want to find. It helps if I say it out loud. And I hold the crystal over the map.

If I'm over the right place, it starts to swing round and round instead of backwards and forwards. Here, I'll show you."

He touched the crystal to the map and then lifted it. "Where is Kenneth Odhar's stone? In Nairn? In Forres?" He moved his hand over the map. The crystal swung straight. At last he sat back, shrugging. "Not today. Not for me, anyway. Would you like to try, Tanya?"

Reluctantly she took the chain, letting it dangle loosely from her fingers. Better get it over with! She held it out, not really watching where she held it. "Where's this stone, then?"

A shock like electricity ran up through the chain. With a yelp she dropped it onto the map and snatched her hand away, rubbing her stinging fingers.

"What happened?" Mr Mandrake was excited.

"Dunno. But I ain't doing that no more, I'll tell yer!"

When they couldn't persuade her to try again, in spite of his disappointment, Mr Mandrake made himself shrug. "Well, it was just a chance."

It was maybe his lack of pressure that persuaded Beth. "I haven't had a shot." She blushed slightly, but put out her hand quite firmly. "I'll give it a bash."

Mr Mandrake chuckled. "Don't bash it too hard, then, you might break it!" Controlling his excitement, he draped the chain over her fingers. "Go ahead."

Concentrating, she held the crystal out over Nairn. "Is this scrying stone here?" The gleam hung steady for a few seconds. Mr Mandrake, eyes narrowed slightly, laid a hand on her shoulder. Almost immediately, the crystal trembled and swayed. In another three seconds, it was clearly moving in a circle.

She turned and gaped up at Mr Mandrake, who was smiling down at her. "Look, it's moving! It's working!"

"We can't be sure yet," he warned her, but still sounding pleased. "Try over some other places, to check."

She tried over half a dozen places, coming back to Nairn twice. Everywhere else, the crystal hung steady or swung in a straight line; over Nairn, each time, it tilted into a circle.

Tanya was astonished. "It's here! Here in Nairn!"

"It certainly looks like it. Well done!" Mr Mandrake patted Beth's shoulder. "You have a rare talent there, my girl!"

She blinked, coming out of her amazement, and scrambled to her feet, beaming proudly. "I'll get a street map - there's one in the lounge. Then we can find out just where it is in the town!"

"Good idea!" As she hurried out, he smiled at the other girl. "Won't be long now, Tanya, until we know where the stone is! Beth's a very powerful scryer. That means she's like a telescope - she can't see by herself, as you might say, but she can help someone else to see much better than usual. I don't know when I've seen..." He sounded, Tanya thought, like a cat that's found the cream. He glanced at her; his greedy voice tailed off, and he tutted to himself. "But that's of no interest to you, is it?"

It certainly was. She was getting more worried by the minute. Okay, so it was exciting. And he'd said it was harmless. Huh! She wasn't so sure. While this old crow had his hand on her shoulder, Beth's face over the map had been blank, mindless almost, as if he was hypnotising her, and now she was all flushed, full of a kind of rapture. Not like her. It was wrong. For Beth, especially; she was too nice and normal. Tanya tried to think, 'That'll teach the stupid girl to mock magic!' but she couldn't.

Beth returned, unfolding the street plan as she came. "Come on!" All eagerness now, she grabbed for the crystal. "Is the stone in the High Street? No... Is it in Seabank Road? No... Is it -"

Mr Mandrake gripped her shoulder, and her gabble stopped with a gasp. He smiled down at her. "Let's maybe save some time," he said. "Where's Firthview House on the map? There. Touch the point on it. Now up. Hold steady, now. Is the stone here?"

The crystal started to circle enthusiastically.

"I've got it!" "Well done, Beth!" Two voices called out together. Tanya didn't shout, but she couldn't help sharing their triumphant grins. They were all laughing.

There was a brisk knock at the door, and it

swung open. Mary stood there, her face furious.

Beth didn't notice. "Now we just have to hunt for it in the house..." Mr Mandrake's finger touched her arm. She stopped and looked round, and turned bright pink.

Mary's lips were tight. "Excuse me for walking in, Mr Mandrake, but I heard the girls." Her voice and expression were icy cold. "We have dinners to see to. Beth, give Mr Mandrake his necklace back and come along. Now, please." Her tone admitted no argument.

"But - but -" Beth was stammering, when Mr Mandrake stopped her.

"You're quite right, Mrs Mackenzie." He gestured to the maps, smiling reassuringly, and scooped the crystal out of Beth's fingers in the same movement. "I shouldn't have kept the girls. We were discussing places of interest. I hope you'll forgive us."

His eyes were very blue, but at that moment Mary was too angry to notice. "I can tell you whatever you want to know about most of the sights in the area. Beth! Tanya!"

Embarrassed and insulted, Beth stood up, trying to keep her dignity. "Excuse us, please, Mr Mandrake."

He smiled to them all, thoughtfully swinging the pendant on its silver chain. "I'll see you around."

Outside, Mary looked straight at the two girls. "Beth, I'm very disappointed in you. I've warned you, over and over, about going into rooms with guests, or taking presents. I want you to stay right away from Mr Mandrake from now on."

"But he's a nice man!" Beth protested. "We were just -"

"I don't care what you were just! I don't want you going behind my back, Beth! Do you hear me?"

Beth looked mutinous, but Tanya shoved her hard towards the stairs. "Right, Aunt Mary. We'll stay right clear of him. Cross me heart an' hope to die. Go on down, Beth. Be wi' yer in a jiff."

As Beth sulkily stomped off down the stairs, Tanya turned to Mary. "Don't worry yer head, Aunt Mary," she hissed. "Wasn't doing no harm. An' I'll keep an eye on her."

"We'll see him off, eh?" She nodded more confidently than she felt, and trotted upstairs to the bathroom.

Mary gazed after her before she shrugged and walked off down the stairs.

Beth was furious. Tanya had better watch out! Whisper about her to her mother behind her back, would she? And get her into more trouble, probably, or say bad things about Mr Mandrake? He was a nice man, he was so, and she'd worked the crystal, not Tanya! Confused and resentful, she got on with the work, crashing the dishes about until her mother's jaw ached from clenching it to hold in her temper.

If they got through dinner without breaking any plates, Mary thought, she'd be astonished... And she wasn't surprised Tanya was keeping out of the way.

Chapter 4

Tanya sat on the side of her bed, arguing with herself for ages. "Can't let Beth get into this. She'll get hurt. Serve her right! No, not really... But what can I do? Tell Aunt Mary? She'd not believe me. An' Beth won't listen, not now. He's a baddie. Yeah. Real bad, smile an' all, like a crocodile." She drew a deep breath. "Gotta stop him. But how?"

There was only one way. She winced as she thought of the sharp jab of power in her hand from the pendulum, but... she had to.

She slipped down to lift a set of Room 3's keys, unseen, and then watched from the top landing until Mr Mandrake went down to dinner. Then she went into his room again.

The lock of the small case couldn't hold out against her skill with a hairgrip. She had the crystal out in less than a minute. With reluctance, she made herself take hold of the chain and concentrate. "Oh, well. Here goes. Where's this stone, then?"

The sharp prickle ran through her fingers again, and she felt a tug towards the door. She was led out, and then, to her surprise, up the stairs, the tingling growing stronger with every step.

It led her to the door of Mary's room. Should she..? She reassured herself, "Ain't pinching nowt. It'll be hidden under a floorboard or in a mousehole. Sure it will."

However, to her dismay she was guided over to the dressing table; to the top drawer. "It's in here! In among Aunt Mary's things." She hesitated... but somehow she had to go on.

Slowly, she lifted out an old chocolate box from the back, behind a pile of scarves. It was full of small bundles of tissue paper. "It's her jewellery. Never thought she'd know about it! Can't stop now, though. This is it, this one!" The sting of the pendulum was actually painful, but as soon as it touched one particular package, the crystal died and dangled, only a pretty trinket. She stuffed it into her shirt pocket and rubbed her fingers.

Then, her hands trembling slightly, she unwrapped the parcel.

On the rustling paper lay a flat stone, an uneven circle about six centimetres across, with a hole through the centre. One side was dark, smooth grey, almost black; the other was almost white, sparkling with mica. She laid it on the palm of her hand. "I've found it."

At the door behind her, Mary asked quietly, "Found what, may I ask?"

Tanya froze.

Woodenly, Mary walked across the room and looked at the bundles of tissue paper left in the chocolate box. Without glancing at the stricken youngster, she said, "Well?"

"Ain't like it seems, Aunt Mary," Tanya whispered. "Honest!"

"Honest?" Mary regarded her for what seemed like a long time. Then she sighed jerkily. "This is why you were so interested in the Brahan Seer. Right. Let me think." Rather blindly, she stuffed away her little box of jewellery, found hairpins and pinned up her slipping chignon again.

Behind her, Beth appeared in the doorway. The work at dinner had, as always, worn away her bad temper. "That's the tea tray up to the lounge, mum - hey, that's better, you were starting to look like Rapunzel - what's wrong? You look awful, mum!"

"I'll - I'll be all right." Mary's knees started to tremble. She sat down on her bed.

Tanya skulked by the door, glaring defiantly at Beth, who was going red. "What is it, mum? Tell me!" What had Tanya done that could make them both look so terrible?

At last, Mary lifted her head. "You asked about the stone at dinner." The youngsters looked at each other. "Beth. Tell me. I want to know what's going on. Why did you ask about the Brahan Seer's stone? No, Tanya. Be quiet."

"The stone? Oh, that's all!" Glad to be able to put things right, Beth happily told all she knew about the stone, and Mr Mandrake's search for it. "And he says it may be worth a lot of money, mum, enough to do all the repairs and alterations! Dry rot and everything! So can we go and see him again after the dishes are all done, to try and find out where in the house it is?"

"You needn't bother." Mary's voice was dry. She lifted a finger to point to Tanya. "She's found it."

"What?" Beth's voice was a squeak. She stared at the stone Tanya held up. She could scarcely believe it. Tanya had found it? By herself? How? Where?

"I had it. If you'd told me all about it like sensible girls, I could have given it to you, without all this carry-on of secrets and magic and - and stealing."

"But - I never knew you had it, mum."

"No?" Mary regarded her rather sourly. "You mean there's something even you didn't know? Alec told me years ago about the family tradition that this was Kenneth's stone. I didn't believe it, but he did. He said it felt uncanny. Apparently his grandfather once saw something in it, but was too frightened to look again. Alec couldn't use it himself, nor Iain, Tanya's father. But when he knew he was dying, Alec told me I was to keep it safe and away from prying scientists and museum-keepers, and pass it on to you, Beth, when you were eighteen."

"Too late, yer better to learn early how to handle magic things, or it don't come as easy." At Mary's cold glance, Tanya bit her lip. "Sorry."

"I nearly told you when you asked about it at dinner, but I thought you were too young." Mary shook her head. "And Tanya came looking for it, rummaging through my things, and found it."

"I'm sorry, Aunt Mary." Tanya's voice, for once, was subdued. "I thought it'd be hidden somewhere…"

"It was."

"Somewhere under a floorboard or something! Not - not where you had it. Were going to give it yer! Just wanted not to let him get it! At least -" she hesitated. What had she intended? "Just - just wanted to find it. I had to, somehow… the dowsing thing - it drew me along. Couldn't stop. But I meant to help!"

"You had no right to go into my room or my drawer. I'm - I'm disgusted, Tanya. And hurt." Mary shook her head. "But I'll accept that you didn't intend to steal from me. Not really." Her expression became even more severe. "I'm angry with Mr Mandrake more than with you. You've been childishly selfish. Arrogant. You didn't care what I'd feel about you going through my private things, taking what belonged to me."

"Didn't think about that." Tanya was angrily ashamed of herself.

"No. I know you didn't. But you should have!" Mary sighed. "All right. You meant no real harm. But he's been - well… I think magic is the use of forces which we don't yet understand. Compasses and marsh lights and rainbows were called magic, until we learned about magnetism and so on. But, at the moment we're like people poking about the back of a TV set, trying to change programmes with a screwdriver. Magic is dangerous. It can derail people's minds. Mr Mandrake had no business getting you involved in even as simple a thing as dowsing without telling me. Give me that pendulum. I'll see him about it later." Her voice was grim as she held out her hand to take the little crystal. "For now - we'd better go down. There's the dishes to do." She turned and marched out. In a while she'd maybe get her feelings sorted out.

Behind her, Beth glared at Tanya. "You'd no business doing that! Going into mum's things! And without me!"

Oh, yeah? Tanya thought. Which was worse? She felt rotten. She stuck the stone in her pocket. Aunt Mary had forgotten to take it back. But she would. What would she do with it?

Beth didn't know what to say. Tanya had raided her mum's chest of drawers; Tanya had upset mum; Tanya was a pest, a rubbishy, disturbing, thieving, sickening pest. But Mr Mandrake said she had power, they both had... She was all confused.

As Mary reached the first-floor landing Mr Mandrake opened the door of Room 3, smiling pleasantly. "I do hope you'll allow the girls to come and talk to me again, Mrs Mackenzie. They charm away my loneliness. Far more interesting than the television."

"I'm sure they are." Mary's tone was cutting, pitched to reach the girls on the floor above. "But I'm afraid not, Mr Mandrake. There'll be no more little sessions with the pendulum. Not while I have anything to say about it. You had no business to involve them in such matters without my permission. So you can scarcely be surprised if I don't trust you with them in future." She held out the pendant to him. "You'll just have to content yourself with the TV."

He smiled as he took the crystal. His eyes were very blue. "But they still need my help, to find what they were looking for."

"The Brahan Seer's stone, you mean?" He blinked. "You mean you need their help. And in any case, you're wrong. Maybe your magic's slipping. They've found it." This time, she was the one to smile at his astonishment. "Oh, yes. I had it all the time. If they'd asked sensibly, straight out, I could have given it to them right away." She nodded in satisfaction, turning to run down the last stairs.

She didn't see the anger in Mr Mandrake's face. But she felt the carpet suddenly stick and lift under her shoes, twisting as if it was actually throwing her down the steep steps. She spun in mid-flight and saw him standing above her, hand raised, the blue of his eyes almost aglow. She crashed against the wall, and down again; her arm cracked between banisters; the agony in it, in her shoulder and head vanished as she blacked out.

At the scream and thud, Beth leapt down the stairs, Tanya right behind her. Mary was crumpled at the foot of the stairs, and Mr Mandrake was running down towards her, calling, "Are you all right, Mrs Mackenzie?"

"Mum!" Beth pushed past him, reaching to tug at her mother's shoulder.

Mr Mandrake stopped her. "No. She's hurt. Look, her wrist's broken." Her right hand was wedged under her at an unnatural angle.

Beth gasped again, then steadied herself and nodded. "Her back could be hurt as well. That's right, don't move her. I'll call the ambulance." She ran for the telephone.

Crouched by Mary's side, Mr Mandrake considered. "Tanya, I believe we could make her more comfortable," he murmured. "Go round to that side, and slip your hands underneath. Ease her up, gently, until I straighten this arm. That's it. Down now, careful. That's better." He checked Mary's pockets while he smoothed her skirt. No stone there. Where was it? Upstairs? How had they found it? And how could he get it? Because he would get it...

Try the easy way first. Keep up the appearance of friendship. It shouldn't be difficult.

Doctor Spalding and the ambulance arrived almost together. While the ambulance men were loading Mary into the ambulance, Doctor Spalding reassured the girls. "Don't worry, now. Her wrist's broken, you know, and her collarbone. I can't say yet about her ankle. But she's starting to stir already. I don't think there's any real damage to the skull or her spine. But you shouldn't have moved her. You could have paralysed her."

Beth gasped. "Oh, no! I told you not to move her, Tanya!"

"No, I'm sure she'll be okay." The doctor smiled encouragingly at Beth. "Are you going in to Raigmore with her, Beth? She'll wake up in the ambulance, I expect."

"Oh! I never thought! I'll get my anorak." Beth hurried off.

The doctor rubbed his chin, and spoke to Tanya. "Now, who's going to look after you?"

She knew what was in his mind but she knew it was hopeless. They were under age... For the first time ever, she suddenly wished she looked more normal. Skull earrings and black nail polish didn't help when you wanted to look respectable and reliable and old.

Mr Mandrake stepped forward, gently reassuring. "I'll keep an eye on things."

Lips pursed, the doctor eyed him doubtfully. "Are you a relative?"

"No, no, just a friend. But a good friend." He smiled warmly at Tanya.

She didn't want to accept his help. "We'll be okay," she snapped defiantly.

"Of course you will, my dear!" Mr Mandrake's tone was silky and patronising, but somehow, in its adult superiority, it soothed the doctor. "Really, there's nothing to worry about, Doctor. In case of any trouble, they'll call on me. Won't you, Tanya?"

Tanya nodded slowly. They needed his assistance - for the moment, anyway. She didn't trust him, not as far as she could throw him, but... "Yeah. Ta."

Beth, racing back, nodded hastily. "Yes, thanks, Mr Mandrake. It's very good of you."

"Have you money? To get home with?" She gaped. "Here." He reached for his wallet and gave her two bank notes. "That'll pay your taxi back. On you go, then, my dear." Absently smiling and thanking him, all her attention on the stretcher bed with her mother on it, she clambered into the ambulance. The doors were shut, and it pulled out of the courtyard and away.

Her obvious familiarity with this man, and the casual way she accepted the gift of money, reassured Doctor Spalding that he wasn't a stranger. It was only for a couple of days, after all. Beth was a sensible lass. And the man's eyes were so blue and kindly... He nodded, climbed into his car and drove off.

Tanya took a deep breath. One danger down, one to go.

Mr Mandrake smiled down at her. People were watching. A day at least before the mother would return. No need to push it. "I'm sure you'll manage beautifully, Tanya." He nodded jovially and went inside.

For a few minutes, Tanya was kept busy

reassuring people about Mary, just a hurt arm, nothing serious, and yes, they could stay, of course they didn't have to move to another hotel. Her face ached with smiling, and her mind ached with watching her language. Eventually the nosiest of them all, Mr Craig, assured her, "I'm absolutely certain, Tanya, you'll look after us just fine. We've got every confidence in you and Beth, haven't we, Babs? Even if Mary doesn't get back for a day or two. And boiled eggs for breakfast, nothing fancy! For everybody, right?" Everybody nodded helpfully. "And if there's anything we can do to help, just ask. Anything at all, we'll be only too glad to, won't we, Babs?" His wife nodded in agreement.

Tanya grinned. "Well, ta, that's great of yer. But we don't need no help just now. Unless yer wants to wash dishes? Neh, just a joke, honest!"

The water in the sink was cold. Draining it, and running the tap to get hot water, Tanya was wondering how long before Beth got back.

A hand touched her arm. She was so startled she jumped, to her embarrassment.

Beside her, Mr Mandrake chuckled gently. "Did I startle you, Tanya? I do apologise. I merely came down to see this marvellous stone. You do have it, don't you?"

His eyes were greedy. She felt chilled, repelled, but drawn to gaze into those cold blue eyes - blue - no! Rebelliously, she tore her gaze away. "Ain't mine. It's Aunt Mary's. See her about it, when she gets back."

"Why not let me have a look at it? It's my job, handling such things, and this is one of the most important undiscovered items around. Naturally I'm interested, my dear."

"No way. I done enough damage, findin' it." She could feel his annoyance building up behind her, and concentrated on filling the sink with near-boiling water. "An' don't call me dear."

There was a pause. She turned off the tap. His hand touched her arm again - and the cup she had carefully filled and kept ready she tossed, the hot water splashing right in his face. "Hah! You keep yer hands off me, see! Or -"

"Or what?" His voice was icy. He dried his face, folded his handkerchief again and put it away carefully. "That was a mistake, Tanya."

"Only mistake I made were listening to you. You an' that stone got me into right trouble."

His lips were tight. "You can get into a great deal more."

She shrugged. "What yer gonna do? Push me down the stairs? Here - was that how Aunt Mary - an' then yer moved her, could've paralysed her -" Shocked, she stared straight at him. His eyes snapped at her - so blue...

"How ridiculous, Tanya! I am your friend." No! That wasn't right! But he reached to hold her wrist lightly. "I showed you the crystal, remember? I'm your friend." She gazed at him helplessly. She had to fight - fight... "And all I ask in return is to see the stone." His touch stilled her, while that cool voice purred, "Calm, Tanya. Relax. I'm your friend. Trust me. I'm your friend. You trust me, don't you?"

Mindlessly, she nodded.

"Good. Good." He sighed in satisfaction. So easy, really. A touch of mental pressure and she was quite overcome. Like taking candy from a baby, as the saying went... The marvellous stone, Kenneth Odhar's scrying stone, was at hand. He could see whatever he wanted, wherever or whenever it was, discover every secret... "You trust me, I'm your friend. So you want to show me the stone. You want to. I'm your friend. Trust me. Show me the stone, Tanya."

Dull, muffled, Tanya's mind mumbled, 'No, don't...' but she couldn't hear it properly... She had to - what? Show him the stone... Yes...

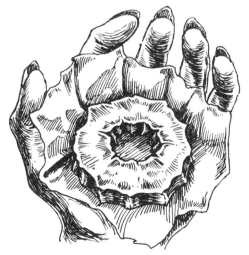

Chapter 5

"Show me the stone, Tanya."

"Yes..." He was a friend... Tanya started to turn towards the pantry.

"Tanya, sweetie pie, Babs and I just decided -" Mr Craig was talking before he had the door fully opened, but hesitated, surprised by their stillness. "What's wrong? Are you all right?"

"Of course she is!" Mr Mandrake snapped. But he had been distracted. Tanya blinked, awakened and tugged away from him.

She swallowed. "Er - yeah. Yeah. We're fine." Just. She drew as far away from Mr Mandrake as possible, rubbing her freezing arm. "Come on in, Mr Craig! An' Mrs Craig! Right pleased to see yer. What can I do for yer?"

The tall, skinny man chattered on happily. "I just thought, my dear, Babs and I just thought, well, we'd just come and give you a hand, with Beth away. Isn't that right, Babs? All these dishes! Far too much for a little girl like you! Though I know you're very good! Why don't you wash, Tanya, I'll dry, and Babs will set the tables ready for the morning?"

"Great!" Tanya turned back to the sink, carefully not looking at Mr Mandrake. He stood undecided for a few seconds in the middle of the floor, and then huffed out. Hah!

The Craigs stayed for over an hour. Tanya kept them as long as she could, as a shield against Mr Mandrake, but at last they gossiped themselves out and up the stairs.

What now?

She had to get the stone away. Ey, lucky that she'd hidden it before starting the dishes - if it had still been in her jeans pocket, she might have just handed it over, before the Craigs came in! She lifted the smallest of the row of teapots. The stone slid out of its hiding place, heavy and cold in her hand. She must hide it better - but where?

Heavy steps sounded on the stairs. He was coming back! She stuffed it in her pocket, snatched up a pan just in case, raced across the dining room to the front hall and glanced round.

Mandrake was standing on the landing above her, on the front stairs. It hadn't been him at the back - or had it?

He smiled. "Ah, Tanya! May I have a word with you? No, wait one moment, my dear," as she snatched at the door handle. "I have an offer to make you."

The door safely open, pan in hand, she paused. He wasn't near her. Do no harm to see what he wanted. "Offer? One I can't refuse, eh?"

So as not to alarm her, he didn't come any closer. "You've had a hard time, Tanya, haven't you?" He sounded sincere and sympathetic. "Your mother - ill." Just in time, he saw by the tightening of her lips that she'd not accept any comments about her mother. "You're so clever that envious fools at school bully you, don't they?"

She glowered. "Like to see 'em try!"

He chuckled. "I'm sure you can stand up for yourself. But I can take you away from squabbles with these ignorant louts. You can be great, Tanya! Great! Yes, you! I have power, you know it, real power! And I can share it with you. I can teach you how to use your power, how to control and develop it, how to make other people obey you, get anything you want. Anything at all, Tanya! Think of it - dream of it!" What would a child want? "Holidays skiing or sailing in the Bahamas? Palaces? A private jet? Fancy clothes? Princes and film stars eager to be your friends? A car like mine? Ten cars like mine?" He was persuasive, urgent. He was smiling. His eyes were blue, and wide.

It was tempting, but... Don't look at his eyes! She could feel the mental pressure slithering in under her defences, and stiffened her resistance to hold him off. Don't trust him...

He came down a step closer. "Tanya, I'm offering you anything! Everything! Join me! I can make you the greatest witch in the world!" Another step.

"An' what's the price, eh? The stone, I suppose." It was burning in her pocket until she felt he must see the glow of it through her jeans.

"That's all. The Brahan Seer's stone. A mere pebble!" Who else deserved the stone, who else had the power to use it fully? He must have it! He struggled to keep the greedy passion out of his voice, to sound light and casual. "So little, in exchange for so much!" Another step.

"Ain't all, though, is it? Yer wants Beth to scry for yer."

He chuckled, sure of her acceptance. "Only if she wants to. But I'm sure she'll soon be happy to join us." With a little bit of helpful persuasion from her friends... "And then I - we - can do anything!" Another step. "Consider, Tanya. Your father and Beth's were brothers. It was pure chance that your father was younger. The stone is your family heirloom too, isn't it? You only met her yesterday. What do you owe her? Give me the stone now, and every secret in the world will be ours, just for the looking." Oh, yes, yes, he must have it! Another step. Only five more...

The seductive pull of his voice, the push of his will, were overpowering. Anything she wanted. Be a real witch. Well, why not? Wasn't it what she'd always dreamed of? That'd show them at school, Miss Snotty Sanderson, and Taffy Bascombe and her gang, and everybody. A proper witch. The chance might not come again...

She was actually reaching for her pocket when Mr Mandrake spoke again, trying to talk as she would. "What can Beth do with it anyway, stupid girl -"

It was what she had thought herself - and she felt guilty. "You think everybody's stupid!" She might have... She'd so nearly... Ey up, dopey, don't hang about, get out while you can! She whirled out to the cool, clean air outside, and ran for her life.

He leapt down the last steps. "Tanya, wait! Stop, Tanya!" His tone firmed, deepened, dominated... "Stop!" The cold, creamy voice dragged her back. His will focused on her, ensnared her. She kept moving, heaving herself across the yard to the gate. Moving was like running in waist-deep water. In treacle. In cement... "Stop! Stop now, Tanya!"

Beth would have submitted, stopped. But Tanya was made of sterner stuff. She kept moving. She shouted at herself, stoking her temper, trying to drown his voice with her own. "Move it! Don't listen! He ain't touching you, so move! Run!"

She did her best. But as the chilling, clinging voice overwhelmed her, she slowed...

A taxi drew up by the gate, and Beth got out, handing money to the driver. "Hello, Tanya! Mum's fine - what's wrong?"

"Him - he's trying to - stop him!" Desperately Tanya jerked it out, reaching out towards Beth with both hands, hoping for help - but what could Beth do?

"What on earth are you doing with that pan?" Beth asked, laughing.

Slowed to a stagger, Tanya fell forwards against the wing of the taxi. Beth caught her. The spell lifted, just a little. She swung round, ready to fight like a rat in a trap, and threw the pan with all her strength.

Mr Mandrake threw up a hand to defend

himself. He stepped backwards, tripped over a tub of geraniums and fell.

Tanya felt the tangle of magic slip from her limbs. She was free! Away round the corner and across the broad spread of the Links she raced, out of earshot of the taxi driver shouting about little hooligans, out of eyeshot of the warlock, running faster and freer as she escaped, panting down under the glowing green and gold sunset to the shelter of the banks of tall grasses beside the shore.

Beth didn't know what was happening. Why was Tanya throwing pans about? Should she stay with Mr Mandrake, calm him down? Or go after Tanya? Surely Tanya must have had a good reason for it? Shocked, she chased her cousin down across the grass.

When the taxi driver helped Mr Mandrake to his feet, rubbing his bruised shoulder and hip, there was no sign of the girls - and his hand was bleeding! They had actually drawn his blood! They'd pay for it! In anger he sent a shaft of power after them, making Beth and Tanya both gasp with a stab of pain in their heads, but then he shrugged. They'd be back... The warlock swept into the house, leaving the driver in mid-sentence. He climbed angrily back into his cab; stuck-up so and so! Maybe the lassie had reason to throw the pan at him!

"What's going on?" Beth demanded as she found her cousin panting in the hollow among the grass.

Tanya grabbed her hands in delight. "Yer okay! An' Aunt Mary? Oh, Beth! Thought he had us, honest! But we done it!"

"Done - did what? What have you done? Apart from knock down one of our guests?"

Tanya rolled over onto her back to stretch the tension out of herself, still breathless. She'd not speak of the offer, for she was ashamed; she had so nearly given in to it... "I saved the stone from him!"

It took a while to convince Beth. She refused flatly to believe in any magical powers, but at length she did accept that he'd been trying to bully Tanya into giving up the stone. "Well, I'd never have thought it of him!" she declared. "So nice and - well, just nice!"

While she muttered to herself, Tanya rolled over and tugged the stone out of her pocket. It was the first time she'd had a chance to look at it properly. "Ain't impressive, is it? Funny, it's blooming cold, not warm, even when it's had me bum sat on it. If it really cures folk, maybe I should borrow it for me mam!" She chuckled. "What d'yer do, eh? Just look through it?" She peered through the small hole in the centre. "Any special side, or -"

She stopped.

"What's wrong?" In surprise, Beth knelt beside her, scared to touch her. "What is it?" Tanya was absolutely rigid, her mouth still open. "Wake up, Tanya!"

She moved, to Beth's relief, and spoke

without taking the stone from her eye. "I can see." It was Beth's turn to freeze. "It's teeny, but clear. Hospital ward. Beds wi' pink blankets, an' machines. Like intensive care. One bed closer up. Woman in it. An' a doctor, speaking to a nurse. She's saying... Can't hear. But she's shaking her head. Pulling the sheet right up. Over the woman's face." She lowered the stone. In the half-light her face shone deathly pale. "Must be Aunt Mary. She's dead!"

Beth snatched the grey stone from her hand, staring at it, and Tanya, in mingled fright, awe and anger. "She isn't! She was fine when I left, nothing wrong with her, only her arm! How did you do that? What did you do?"

"Oh! Aunt Mary!" Tanya was biting her lip. "I brung it on her! Killed her! If I hadn't thought to use the crystal to find the stone, she'd be alive now! Aunt Mary! Aunt Mary!" She was near hysterics.

"Don't be stupid!" Beth shouted. In spite of herself, she half-believed Tanya had seen something. But it couldn't be her mother - it couldn't! "Mum's fine, I tell you! I'm not staying to listen to this! It's nonsense! Nonsense!" Ignoring the distress in Tanya's face, Beth pushed herself to her feet and ran back towards the house. After ten steps, she turned and threw the stone back to thud on the sand at Tanya's feet.

Shuddering, shaken by dry sobs, Tanya watched her go. It didn't matter. Nothing

mattered. Aunt Mary. Nice, kindly Aunt Mary...
Cool, silver ripples hushed, hushed gently on
the long sand, but they didn't calm her. A
scalding horror of guilt burned through her.
She'd killed Aunt Mary! She pressed her fists to
her mouth to stop herself screaming. She'd
seen the body -

A body. She'd seen a body. Desperately she
grasped at the new thought. She hadn't seen the
face. She didn't know who it was. It could be
anybody. Anybody at all. Herself, even. In the
future. It didn't have to be Aunt Mary. The
relief was enormous.

After a minute she looked round, feeling
something missing. Where was Beth? Gone.
Yes, hadn't she run off? She swallowed and
blinked, trying to remember. What had she
said? About Aunt Mary. Beth would be going
spare. And no wonder. And she'd gone back -
alone! With the Mandrake man there...

At least she'd left the stone. There it was, a
glowing ring of white in the pale light. Tanya
bent to pick it up. It still felt cold. She buried it
deep into her pocket again.

Beth might need her... Stupid Beth - no!
She'd not say that again, that was what he'd
said... Tanya didn't want to go back, but she
had to. She was freezing, anyway, her bare arms
covered in goosebumps in the sharp evening
breeze. Her fists clenched tight. If that
Mandrake tried to lay a finger on her, or on
Beth, she'd - she'd break it!

The kitchen light was still on. She was shattered after the long day's excitements, but there was a solid, dull temper about her as she marched straight across the car park. Halfway over, she kicked something that clattered; the pan. Right! She grabbed it. Anybody waiting for her had better look out. She threw open the kitchen door, jaw set like a terrier ready for a fight.

It wasn't Mr Mandrake.

Beth was sitting in her mother's chair, crying bitterly. She had been so upset she'd phoned the hospital again, and yes, her mother was doing fine, but she couldn't be sure, not now, not after Mr Mandrake saying Tanya had power, and she'd found the stone, and maybe what she'd seen would come true...

Tanya's temper collapsed like a sandcastle in the tide of her guilt. "Oh, Beth! I must've made a mistake - it weren't Aunt Mary I seen in the stone, can't've been. Don't cry, Beth! Please don't cry! I'm sorry, honest I am! An' I'm sorry for finding the stone without yer, an' - an' - I'm just sorry!" To her horror, she found herself crying too. She knelt in front of Beth; holding her hands, sobbing until Beth finally started to hug her, to comfort her; and was comforted in turn.

They both felt better for it.

"Gotta get some sleep, or we won't be fit for nowt tomorrow. What we gonna do wi' the stone?" Tanya asked eventually, sniffing violently. She washed her face at the sink and dried it on a tea towel.

Beth blew her nose hard, on a paper hankie. "Can't we just take it upstairs? Put it under your pillow or something?"

"No way. He'd come looking for it."

Beth could scarcely credit this, but she sighed, too tired to argue. "Hide it, then."

"Where?" The teapot was scarcely safe enough, Tanya felt. But there was something... She tried to remember what Cat had said one day... "Iron. That's it. Iron stops spells. Specially if it's magnetic. But any iron'll do at a pinch."

"Oh?" Beth shrugged. "So find some - here, I've got an idea." She rummaged in the pantry. "Here's mum's old cast-iron pans. We never use them, they're too heavy. Put it in the big one, with another one on top, and then the lids. And then stuff it away under the shelf behind the vegetable rack. If you really want to wrap it up in iron, that's the best I can think of for tonight."

It was the best Tanya could think of, too. She laid the stone down inside the pan. It seemed to stick to her hand, not wanting to part from her - but she shook it off and sighed with relief as the next pan cut it off from her sight. Phew!

"That's that, then." Beth yawned wearily. "I'm for bed. Coming, Tanya?"

"In a minute."

Beth went to the door, and then hesitated. She had to say it. "I should - I mean - well, just thanks, Tanya. I couldn't manage here, not just now, without you being here. I don't mean Mr

Mandrake - he's part of it, but just - with mum hurt, and so on - I'm glad you're here."

She almost ran out, before Tanya could shut her mouth enough to thank her. Well, at last. She was useful, wanted. That was one for the books, right enough!

Tanya stretched her aching back and shut the pantry door. Nobody'd look in there among the potatoes and stuff for a magic stone, anyway. It was after eleven, not late by her standards, but she was shattered! Well, she'd done a lot today. A coke would go down a treat. She opened the fridge.

Mr Mandrake came into the kitchen, smiling.

Oh, not again!

Rather to her surprise, she found that she didn't care. She opened the coke with a bright hiss to echo her sharp sigh. "It's gone."

His smile vanished. "Gone?"

She felt a glow of pleasure at his frustrated glare. "Yeah."

"Where?"

As if it had been in her mind all along, the answer came to her. "In the quarry. Remember, where yer picked us up this morning? Beth nipped along just now an' tossed it in, among a hundred old cars an' junk, all rusty. An' magnets in 'em, too. An' she says it's all gonna be filled in next week. So yer can't get it now." He actually snarled at her. She smiled slightly. "An' yer can forget yer unrefusable offer, an' all. Ain't interested. I'll be a witch some day, right enough, but not wi' your help."

He was dangerous, of course, especially now, when she'd beaten him. She still wasn't afraid, though. "You touch me an' I'll break yer fingers, an' scream like a fire siren - an' I can. The Craigs is just upstairs."

She nearly laughed at his expression. A twelve year-old, talking to a grown-up like this? To *him*? But she didn't care. Just don't look at his eyes. "Try any funny stuff, magic or that, an' I'll curse yer. An' it were you as said I had power. Right? So what'll it be?"

His face, she was pleased to see, was a picture; astonishment, anger, insult. "Well!" he said finally, almost in admiration. "This is a change, Tanya. What's got into you?"

"I'm worn out, that's what. An' fed up to the back teeth wi' you. An' me back's killing me. I ain't got no energy for no nonsense." Her tone was flat.

He nodded, considering her venomously. "All right, my dear. You've outfoxed me. And you don't want to join me."

"No."

He shrugged. He'd not lower himself to shout at this little horror. But he wasn't used to being crossed, even by important, powerful people, let alone a scruffy guttersnipe like this. And his hip was still sore. He felt fury boiling inside him at the disappointment. She must be punished.

His calm face was belied by the violent rage in his eyes, the white tension round his mouth. "Very well, Tanya. It's your own decision.

Remember that in the future. It's your choice, your own doing. You and your cousin have defied me, caused me actual injury, and removed something that I particularly wanted. So you'll not be surprised if I feel somewhat irritated."

"Feel any way yer want. I'm going to bed." She walked past him. She was ready to scream, as she had threatened, but he didn't touch her. She felt a warm triumphant glow spreading through her insides. They'd beaten him! The stone was safe. Aunt Mary was okay. Whoever that had been in the hospital bed, it wasn't her. She'd just have to wait and see. It was true, she knew it was true. She'd find out what it meant some day. But in the meantime, she wasn't just a pest. She was useful, needed. Wanted.

And she was the one who'd seen through the stone. Magic!

Yes, it was.

Who could it have been, in the hospital?

Oh, stuff that. And stuff the Mandrake man. Bed.

Beth was asleep already. The bedroom was still tidy. The contents of the drawers were disturbed, to her annoyance. He'd been in here, searching for the stone, while they were out. At least the things weren't all over the floor. They felt disgusting, dirty and slimy, as if they'd had a slug crawling over them. But that was daft. Tanya locked the door, jammed a chair under the handle for extra security, and fell asleep quickly.

THE SEER'S STONE

Chapter 6

Tanya woke slowly, muttering in annoyance. She felt cold, yet sweaty. What had wakened her? A noise? No, all was quiet. A movement? Nothing stirred anywhere... Not even Beth's breathing. She was chilled even further. There was absolutely nothing, nothing but darkness, all around her. No streetlight, no line of brightness under the door. Nothing but black.

What had happened? How had she got here, wherever it was?

Mandrake had done something...

There was something moving in the black. Something huge. She could feel it breathing; feel the icy chill from its slimy skin. Slowly it squelched, slurped, oozed closer and closer. If it was light, she'd see it. In the dark, it was invisible...

Her heart was pounding. She was desperate to escape but she couldn't; clammy tentacles were clamped tightly round her, clinging, binding, smothering. She couldn't move, couldn't breathe... choking...

With a huge effort, she surged upwards, screaming.

The yellow curtains glowed soft gold in the first dawn light. Beth was snoring slightly in the next bed. Nothing else was in the room. She must have screamed in silence.

A nightmare.

72

Three o'clock. Four hours until she had to get up, and she felt dreadful. Exhausted and cold. Her duvet was mostly on the floor, and the rest tangled tightly round her legs, sticky and unpleasant. She tugged it into place and lay down again, rubbing at goosebumps on her thin arms. Put on the fan heater? No, the noise might wake Beth. She shivered resentfully for nearly an hour before she fell asleep again.

Beth became slowly aware of... ohh... cold... Dozily she rolled over and looked round. There was a mist rolling under the door, glowing eerie greenish-white. Like dry-ice mist in a pantomime, with Mr Mandrake as the Demon King, she thought, smiling. But... this was summer. Panto's were at Christmas...

Something wrong...

She sat up. Tanya was sleeping quietly. The mist had covered the floor, and was swirling softly round the beds. It was unnatural. She reached down to touch it. Her hand was shocked with a terrible chill, a strike of cold so icy that a pain shot up to her heart. She called out to wake Tanya, but no sound came out. She shouted, screamed, but in helpless silence. Her cousin didn't move. She couldn't get off the bed to go and shake Tanya; she didn't dare put a foot into this freezing mist. But it was rising all the time, lapping like a rising tide at the edge of the bed. It would spill over, freeze Tanya soon; she had to wake her, get her out of here! She forced herself up to kneel on the bed, grab her pillow to toss it over...

How could she kneel on her bed? It was right under the low slope of the ceiling. She even had to be careful how she sat up, never mind kneeling. This wasn't right...

She looked more closely, rubbing her eyes.

She was sitting up, not kneeling. No mist round the beds, only shadow, from the morning light. Just a bad dream. She rolled back onto the pillow, sighing in relief.

What time was it? Five o'clock, nearly. Wearily she got up and looked out; it was light already, but grey, with a steady drizzle. Shivering, she wondered about putting on the heater, but the noise of the fan would wake Tanya. She huddled down into her bed, wishing she had an electric blanket. It was nearly six before she fell asleep.

When the alarm clock finally sounded at six-thirty, they were both heavy-eyed and still tired. Tanya switched the fan heater to its highest setting before even turning off the buzz. "By 'eck, I'm frazzled! Never felt as bad! Nightmares all night! An' colder than the Arctic!" She shuddered as she rotated in front of the warm blast.

Still half-asleep, Beth nodded, struggling with her hair. "Me, too. It was like - like being in a deepfreeze. Horrible. I'd've got up and put on the heater, but I didn't want to risk waking you." She sounded peeved.

"Me too." Tanya protested defensively. "Thought o' getting meself a cuppa, but I didn't want to - well, to go down the stairs. Not wi' him down there."

"Who? Oh, Mr Mandrake? Don't start that again!" But Beth grimaced. "You know, in my dream, I thought it was him who made me so cold."

"Me an' all." Tanya agreed glumly.

"Funny we felt the same. Guilty consciences!" Beth tried to cheer up. "Maybe it's just the weather. It was raining earlier." She rose to peer out of the window and made a face. "Still is. Ouch! I can't get the tangles out of my hair this morning. I must've been tossing about - I don't usually have this trouble. Ow! Would you look at that, my comb's snapped! Oh, come on, let's have a quick shower to wake up."

"An' warm up! Still perishing."

Beth groaned. "I can feel it. This is going to be one of those days."

While they finished laying the tables, Tanya told Beth her suspicions about Mary's fall, and was annoyed when Beth laughed disbelievingly. "What an imagination!" she jeered. "Mum said she was halfway down the stairs before she started to fall. He couldn't have pushed her. And all that carry-on last night - well!" She pushed a strand of hair back and grinned nastily. "What did he do? Ask you to let him see the stone. Big deal! Why not let him, eh? All this about his hands freezing you - horror, horror! Return of the Son of Frankenstein! When I think how cold I was last night, in my bed, I'm not surprised his hands were chilly! Hitting him with a pan, for heaven's sake! We'll be lucky if he doesn't charge you with assault!"

Tanya couldn't express the menace, the power, the commanding chill that had held her captive. Beth just laughed. "Honest, just because the man's got a whatsisname, a pendulum for dowsing, you're hooked on this witchcraft idea. You'll be saying next that he put a curse on us both to give us those nightmares!"

"Wouldn't put it past him," Tanya muttered.

"Oh, give over. Sorry I mentioned it. Have you put the butters out? Oh, well done!"

Tanya's face darkened at Beth's patronising tone.

Beth bit her lip. "Sorry, Tanya. I'm just bad-tempered this morning."

"Me an' all! Right narky, the pair o' us." Tanya looked thoughtful. "Him again?"

"Oh, give it a rest!" Beth snapped. But when she thought about it, she wasn't usually this uptight... It was just worry, with mum being away. "Get out the eggs, will you? There's the urn boiling, and the pan for the eggs, and it's still ten to. At least we're in good time!"

The guests weren't. They straggled down late, at intervals, yawning and irritable, only speaking to complain that the dining room was cold. The big heater blasting away in the corner made no difference to the chill. Nothing pleased them. The cornflakes were soft, the toast was too light or too dark, the eggs were runny or stone-hard, the butter wouldn't spread, the milk was off, the jam was too thick, was there no apple juice...

They ate in a solid gloom, grumbling unhappily within their family groups, without the usual cheery breakfast chatter between the tables, until someone mentioned she'd had a nightmare. Then they all joined in; bad dreams, suffocation, headaches, a cold and clammy feeling. One man had switched his electric blanket on and fallen asleep, to wake again soaked in sweat. "Lucky I didn't electrocute myself!" Even Mr Craig wasn't his normal chirpy self.

When Beth asked as usual who would be in for dinner, there was a general depressed fidgeting. "I don't think we'll stay, dear," one lady said. Everybody nodded. "Not when your mother's ill. You'll be wanting to go visiting, won't you? We think we'll just be on our way." In the end, as if they were glad to escape, everyone except the Craigs was leaving, even the ones who had been booked in until the weekend.

Tanya glowered. This sympathy for Beth and her mum was just an excuse.

Beth frowned her to silence, smiled and nodded. "I'll get your bills ready, then."

Tanya sniffed as she stacked dirty dishes. "Just exactly why's everybody off, eh?"

"Well, it happens." Working out bills, Beth was glum. "But we've got a lot to do now. All those beds to change. Oh, well, I suppose we'll cope. He'll be down in a minute. You clear the rest of the tables, will you, while I get these done. Didn't the Sinclairs have packed lunches yesterday?"

When Mr Mandrake appeared he smiled charmingly. "Well, Tanya! Did you sleep well? And the rest of the guests?" There was an odd significance in his tone.

She regarded him accusingly. "Knew it! I knew it!"

"You knew what, my dear?"

"It were you! You made us have them dreams!" Her voice rose.

In the kitchen, Beth was putting Mr Mandrake's coffee into his coffeepot. What was Tanya up to now? Angrily, she started to go through to the dining room, but Mandrake's next words stopped her.

"You shouldn't have crossed me, my dear." He smiled at Tanya. "You should have taken your chance when it was offered. Such a pity. You have enormous potential. So has your cousin. But now it'll all go to waste."

He sighed in angry resignation. "You see, I happen to be one of the chief wizards of Britain. An Ipsissimus, if you know what that means? The father of all magic. So when I felt drawn to this area, to this particular house, I knew there must be something special here. And there was.

You, my dear, and Beth, and this stone of yours. You are practically ringing with power, like a burglar alarm, to those who can hear."

Tanya stopped herself glancing round at the kitchen door. She hoped that this 'ringing' she was apparently doing would blank out any sense of the stone's nearness.

"With you two and the stone under my control, I'd have had more power than you can dream of. But you have thwarted me. It might have been intriguing to force you, compel you to serve me. I could do it, but - no. You have just too much potential to be trained safely. Especially working with your cousin. And Beth wouldn't come to me without you. And now the stone has gone, too. Your stupid, childish obstinacy has damaged my plans, my dear. And you dared to attack me personally. I have taken the liberty of retaliating. I've made a tiny change in the house."

His smile spread viciously. "Cold, isn't it? Depressing. Bad-tempered. And it'll stay that way. You'll never again heat it up, make it the nice, warm, happy house it was." He beamed at her, smug and satisfied. "And without the skills I could have given you, you'll not be able to remove the spell. Nobody will ever be happy here again!"

Tanya stood and stared at him. "Yer mean - you've done something to the house, to ruin Beth an' Aunt Mary, put a curse on it, just because we wouldn't give yer the scrying stone?" She shook her head in disbelief. "Yer an evil snake!"

He snorted in amused annoyance. "What a charming image! A snake, yes, but -"

"No." She gazed at him in disgust, her lip curling. "Snakes is natural. You're just big-headed an' greedy an' arrogant an' - an' slimy, clear through. An' yer made yerself that way. Nobody else to blame."

"And I thought you were nice." Beth stepped through the doorway from the passage. "But you're not. You're -" She paused, trying to think of exactly what she meant. She felt - hurt. Upset. Disappointed. In him, and herself for believing in him - and in her liking for him, that had turned sour. She was normally polite, but suddenly her temper swelled.

"Crazy," Tanya suggested.

Beth shook her head. "No. Not crazy."

Mr Mandrake's smile was wary. "Thank you, my dear."

"All smiley and smarmy on top, but a spoiled bully underneath."

"Smarmy? Spoiled bully?" Mandrake's voice was high and incredulous.

"Spoiled rotten." Tanya watched him in some satisfaction.

"How dare you!" He seemed to swell in his anger.

Beth tried not to show how cold and frightened she suddenly felt. She understood now what Tanya had been trying to tell her.

Tanya tensed. "I'll yell!" she warned him. "Folks'll hear me!"

As if to prove her words, a lady came in from the front hall, rummaging in her shoulder bag. "Ah, Beth, can we pay you now?" She looked from the girls to Mr Mandrake, sensed trouble, and started to back out, bumping into her husband who was entering behind her. "Er - sorry..."

"No, no. Come right in, please, Mrs Harris," Beth urged her. Their rescuers hovered uncertainly. Keep it looking normal... "Tanya, will you see to Mr Mandrake's breakfast?"

"What? Me? Oh. Yeah. Yeah, right." Finally getting the message from Beth's eyebrows, Tanya agreed amiably, but with a malicious gleam in her eye. "Right, then. How many eggs, Mr Mandrake? An' how d'yer want 'em? Soft or hard? Coffee, isn't it?" And whatever he asked for, he'd get the opposite. Burnt toast, tea...

Maybe he read her mind. "Nothing, thank you. I'm leaving right away."

Beth almost gasped with relief. "I'll get your bill ready, too, then."

"What?" His jaw dropped, as if he wasn't used to being asked to pay for anything. "Hmph! Very well. I'm sure you'll need the money. Soon, my dear, if not immediately."

Beth firmed her chin. How dare he! "If you'll excuse me, then, I'll see to Mr and Mrs Harris first." She made herself smile, and turned towards the couple who were leaving.

Mr Mandrake smiled too. "Do attend to business, my dear. While you still have it! Don't forget to deduct the money I lent you last night!" He stalked out.

Mr Harris stared after him. "Jeez! What a - a -"

"Yeah." Tanya forced herself to shrug. "Get all sorts."

The phone rang in the hall. "I'll get it." Tanya turned away, while Beth wrote out the receipt, smiled, hoped Mr and Mrs Harris enjoyed the rest of their holiday -

"Beth." Tanya was holding out the telephone. "Hospital. About yer mam."

"What is it? Excuse me, please." The Harrises stood eavesdropping. "This is Beth Mackenzie. What's happened?" Her voice shot up. "But she was all right last night! She was speaking to me... But... Yes. Yes, I'll come right away." She stared at Tanya as if she was half stunned. "It's mum. She's worse. She's gone into a coma. Something about concussion, possible brain damage. They want me to go in straight away."

Chapter 7

"I'll call yer a taxi." Tanya took the telephone out of Beth's slack hand, looked for the number on the list above the phone, and dialled.

The Harrises left, full of sympathy, eager to spread the news. Beth stood unable to think, helplessly unsure as to what to do for the best. "But I can't go! Who'll look after the house?"

"Oh never mind the house. Yer mam's more important. She needs yer, so go!" Tanya urged. "I'll see to things here." She turned to the phone. "Hello? Can we have a taxi, urgent, at Firthview Guesthouse? What? Half an hour? But it's an emergency!" She put down the phone, shrugging apologetically "That's the best they can do, they say. Ey, here's somebody else wanting to pay. You sort 'em out, an' do the rest o' the bills while I get yer coat."

By the coat rack in the back hall, Tanya suddenly stopped dead. She knew something that might help... No. It wasn't possible.

Mr and Mrs Craig came down the stairs. "What's wrong, Tanya? You're white as a sheet, dear! What's happened?"

"Beth's mam's had a relapse, an' the hospital wants her in, pronto. An' the taxi can't come for half an hour."

They were both upset by the news. "Oh, dear! I'd take her," Mr Craig fussed, "but our car's in the garage, I had a little bump the day we arrived. Such a pity! Oh, dear!"

"It's okay," she reassured him. "She'll get there quick enough. Like to go meself, but," she shrugged, "somebody's got to mind the place."

"Oh, yes, of course. Never mind, I'm sure it'll be -"

"Harold!" Mrs Craig's voice, that Tanya had only heard once or twice before, agreeing mildly with her husband, was suddenly brisk and businesslike. "Your insurance covers you for driving any car, doesn't it? Take Mary's car. Then they can go, right away. I know taxis, if they say half an hour they mean at least three quarters. You'd be there long before then." Tanya opened her mouth to protest. "Don't worry, dear, I'll see to everything. I'll tell you a secret, my dear - I don't really like holidays, having nothing to do. And my daughter does bed and breakfast, so I know the routine. Don't you worry about a thing."

"Oh, what a good idea, Babs! Come along, then, Tanya. Now, what will we need? Coats, and the car keys, well, you'll get them, of course, and -"

"Harold! Hurry!"

"Yes, dear! Just going!"

Mr Craig wasn't used to a big car. "It's not the same as mine, dears," he smiled after a particularly solid slam on the brakes stopped the big estate just millimetres short of a lorry. "It'll take me a little time to get used to it."

"No sweat, Mr Craig!" Beth smiled automatically.

84

Tanya opened her eyes to glance at her cousin, and swallowed with difficulty. "Speak for yerself!" she muttered.

In shock, Beth was talking absently. "It's very heavy on the wheel, mum said - says. I wouldn't know, I've only driven a tractor."

Tanya leaned forwards over the back of the seat. "You've driven a tractor? Honest?"

"Oh, yes. Just driving round the fields, not out on the road." Beth shrugged, quite matter-of-fact. "On a farm you learn all sorts of things. I can mend a puncture, and use a shotgun, and gut and skin a rabbit."

Tanya made a face. "Yegh! Don't fancy that, killing a rabbit!" But she was fascinated. This was a side of prissy, gentle, polite Beth that she'd never imagined.

"I shot a roe deer once."

"Yer never!"

"Somebody had to." Beth pursed her lips against the disapproval radiating from Tanya and Mr Craig. "They were raiding the peas, and dad borrowed a pal's rifle and took me out."

"Just for a few peas?" Tanya demanded. "Deer's smashing. Cried me eyes out when Bambi's mam got shot."

"Bambi?" Beth snorted. "Cutesy Hollywood rubbish! Smashing's about right. They were wrecking our fields, hundreds of pounds of damage. And farmers can't insure against deer. I killed a buck with one shot. Roast venison's delicious."

"How could yer? Never took you for cruel!"

"No." Beth shook her head, glad of the distraction. "You mustn't kill for fun, or for show, just for food or self-protection, dad always said. Causing any pain you don't absolutely have to, that's what's cruelty." Like Mr Mandrake.

Tanya shrugged. "Still don't think it's right, killing."

"D'you think sausages grow on trees? Everything dies sometime. Plants, animals, people. Even vegetarians kill things. It's been proved scientifically, plants can feel and remember and so on. So which is worse, killing one deer or a field full of potatoes?"

Tanya couldn't answer that. Beth was pleased to have got the last word for once.

"Well!" Mr Craig was quite shocked. "I must say, I'd not have thought it of your mother. Fancy, a girl of your age going shooting. It's not ladylike."

"Watch out!" Tanya yelped. With a wild wrench at the steering wheel, Mr Craig attended to his driving again, and in a huff, scarcely spoke for the rest of the trip.

Everything dies sometime... But not yet! Reminded of her mother, Beth tried to send her a mental message of love and reassurance, and also desperate need. 'Mum, you're going to get better, you'll be all right! I love you! Mum, you've got to be all right! What'll I do without you?'

Behind her, Tanya fondled the scrying stone, rubbing her thumb to and fro across the smooth surface, praying that it would work. Was it really Aunt Mary, then, that she had seen in the stone? Would they be too late? At least the Mandrake man didn't know about them. About the stone being here. That was one good thing.

Back at Firthview, Mr Mandrake was just finishing his leisurely packing. He locked his cases, picked them up and strolled downstairs into the hall. It had stopped raining; he'd have a pleasant drive south. How cheap of Beth, to insist on him paying! He wouldn't dream of cheating them. They'd need it all. He had, after all, done far, far worse to them. He smirked as he rang the bell.

He was surprised when Mrs Craig came out into the hall. "Yes? Oh, your bill, Mr Mandrake! Beth left it here somewhere - yes, here it is. Yes, a cheque's fine, I'm sure."

As he signed his cheque, he asked casually, "Has Beth gone out, then?"

"Yes. Off to the hospital. I'm afraid her mother's had a relapse. It sounds serious, too. A coma, she said."

"A relapse? Oh, dear!" He tried to look sympathetic. Young Tanya must be wishing she'd listened to him, and could ask for his help now. Too bad; too late. Or was it? She might be more easily persuaded now. But could he trust her in the future? He could bind her in various ways. He'd done it with others, now his terrified slaves back in London. But with her power, once she could control it, and her wilfulness, she'd end up a rival, not an assistant. No, safer - better not. No, of course he wasn't afraid of the brat.

Mrs Craig, relieved of her husband's stream of chatter, was making the most of her freedom. "I just told Tanya to go along with Beth, and I'd see to the house. She had a good luck charm that she thought might help. So superstitious, modern children, aren't they?" She didn't like him, and was glad to see the back of him. "Date, amount, signature, all correct. Thankyou, that's just grand! Goodbye, then. Drive carefully, and enjoy the rest of your holiday!"

He had smiled his thanks and was carrying his cases out of the door when what she had said struck him. He almost dropped the cases, swinging round in a hurry. "Did you say - Tanya had a charm?"

"Yes." She was puzzled, slightly alarmed by his urgency.

"What was it like?" He waited, breathless.

"A kind of stone ring - "

"They've gone to Inverness Hospital? You're sure, woman?" His eyes were piercing blue.

Flustered, insulted, she bridled. "Yes. But there isn't an Inverness Hospital. Or rather, there's three or four. Raigmore, and the Royal Northern, and Craig Dunain, and -"

"More than one? There's more than one hospital up here?"

"Yes, indeed!" She was really insulted now,

his influence fading as the force of her own annoyance grew. "You Londoners all think civilisation stops at the Watford Junction -"

That lying little madam, Tanya! Thought herself so clever, did she, deceiving him - he'd make her suffer for it! The stone was still here, still within reach! They'd taken it to try to cure the Mackenzie woman, he knew it. "Think!" he commanded Mrs Craig, dropping a case and grasping her arm. "You know this godforsaken part of the world. I don't. Which hospital was she taken to? Where did they go?" His eyes were blue...

"Where?" Mrs Craig's mind went blank. "Er - Raigmore. Yes, I'm sure it was."

Raigmore Hospital. Yes, that sounded familiar. He let her go, leaving her to recover slowly, rubbing at her arm in mixed fright, anger and shock. He strolled out to his car, slung the cases in the boot, slid into the driver's seat and pressed the button to lower the roof. The rain had stopped; the sun was just coming out; the world was fresh and bright and full of joy. It was going to be a wonderful day... The engine started with a deep snarl, like a tiger; he always enjoyed the sound of power, and this morning he especially relished it. Today, the tiger would sink its claws in deep! He laughed in delight. How melodramatic!

When he got his hands on that cheeky brat... Gravel scattered. The long car skidded out of the yard, tyres screeching.

Mr Craig jolted round the last roundabout and turned in to Raigmore Hospital. "I'll let you off at the patients' entrance. Here we are. My, that was close! These ambulances do take up so much room! I'll go and find a parking space, my dears, and then wait for you in the cafeteria. I need a cuppa, after that drive!"

Not the only one, Tanya thought.

Tanya couldn't help grinning when Beth said, "Thank-you," automatically to the automatic doors. Typical Beth! She followed Beth at a trot to the lift, and then along to the ward.

Mary's bed was empty.

"She's gone!" Beth was white.

"Don't be soft, Beth! Calm down!" Round the corner, a nurse was writing at a desk. "Where's Mrs Mackenzie? This is her daughter Beth. We was asked to come in. What's happened?" They mustn't be too late.

The nurse gave them a professional, reassuring smile. "Don't worry, dear, we've just moved her to Room 4 so she wouldn't be disturbed. You wait here, I'll go and see if Doctor Arkwright's free to speak to you."

While Beth peered anxiously after the nurse, Tanya was looking around. "Ey up, there's Room 4!" She hurried towards it, tense with fright.

"We can't burst in!" Beth tried to stop her, but she had the door open already. Beth nervously followed her in, not noticing as she sagged at the knees with relief. The coverlets were blue, not pink.

Mary was very pale, lying absolutely motionless. A notice was fastened to the head of the bed; NOTHING BY MOUTH. Her arms lay on the covers, the right in plaster, the left with a drip-feed attached.

Beth moved round to the far side of the bed to take her mother's left hand, whispering, "Mum! Mum, it's me, Beth! Can you hear me, mum?"

Mary didn't move.

The nurse came in, looking annoyed. "I thought I said -" Looking at Beth's tearless white face, she shook her head. "Never mind, dear. At least you're not the hysterical sort."

"No - no..." Beth muttered.

"No, and just as well, too. Pull that chair forwards for her, lassie. Sit down, dear."

An elderly doctor appeared. The nurse greeted him with a shake of her head. He took Mary's pulse, looking grave. "I'm Doctor Arkwright." His eyes winced from Tanya to Beth. "Are you Mrs Mackenzie's daughter?"

"Yeah, she is." Tanya answered him. "An' I'm her cousin, Beth's that is. I'm Tanya. What's going on? What's happened?"

Doctor Arkwright looked at them doubtfully. "Is there no adult - no uncle or aunt who could come? A neighbour? Nobody at all?"

"Ain't nobody else. Just us." Tanya was getting angry. "For crying out loud -"

The doctor shrugged, accepting it, but spoke deliberately to the respectable girl.

"Well, Beth, your mother is in a coma. You know what that means?"

Typical grown-up, talking down to the kiddies, Tanya thought. "What is it, a brain haemorrhage? From the fall last night, eh?"

"It could be, er, Tanya." Rather taken aback by the expertise, he gave more information than he'd meant to. "We've taken X-rays and scans, but unfortunately they don't show us anything, and her pulse is steadily growing fainter. I'm afraid we're going to have to put her on a ventilator very shortly." He looked across at the nurse. "Will you warn Intensive Care, Nurse Jones? They're expecting her, and we can't leave it much longer." He glanced down. "In fact, I'm glad you called me. Get a porter to move the bed down now."

The nurse nodded. "Right away. Don't worry, Beth," she said kindly as she went out. "We're doing all we can."

Tanya sniffed. "If yer dunno what's wrong, what can yer do?" she demanded.

"Oh, there's a lot we still haven't tried," the doctor replied cheerfully. "The ventilator's what the films call a life support machine. It'll give us time to do more tests. We'll find out what's wrong. And sometimes a good rest is all people need to heal themselves."

Tanya bit her lip. She didn't believe a word of it. Aunt Mary could be in this coma for ages - forever... How could they get rid of him? He'd not let them try the stone on Aunt Mary, that was for sure! And once she was in Intensive Care, she'd be watched all the time, it'd be impossible...

The doctor was saying, "Now, Beth, I want you to speak to her, try to get through to her. But don't be too upset if it doesn't work -" His bleeper sounded suddenly. "I must go and phone in," the doctor said. "Go ahead, Beth, talk away."

Beth leaned forwards. "Wake up, mum! Come on, wake up! It's me, Beth!"

"That's it." The doctor turned to Tanya. "The porter will be along for her soon."

"Ta." Tanya nodded agreeably as he left. But no sooner had the door closed behind him than she was tugging out the stone from her pocket. "Here's our chance!" She dived towards the sink in the corner, to get a glass of water.

Beth didn't move.

"What's wrong?"

Her cousin shook her head doubtfully. "It's no use. It won't work. Maybe in the past, when people believed in it, but not now!"

Tanya's shoulders slumped. "Oh, that's all we need, Beth, you losing yer nerve!" But then her defiant, stubborn temper shot up. She snarled at her cousin, "Well, I ain't giving up, even if you are! What we got to lose? An' we got yer mam to win!" She glared across the bed in furious frustration. "It can cure folks. It can - you know it can. Yer dad said so. So come on! You take the glass. We got to dip the stone in the water -"

"It's not holy water," Beth objected, reluctantly taking the glass Tanya held out.

Tanya moaned. "Come on! Can't expect everything to be perfect." Beth wasn't convinced. "Look, I'll bless it, then, an' that'll make it holy water." How did you bless water? She held her pendant cross the right way up, over the glass, and looked upwards in urgent pleading. "God bless this water, please, amen." She dipped the cross in the water.

She hadn't meant to do anything, except keep Beth happy, to help the stone to work. But a feeling of warmth, of zinging strength and comfort filled her and flowed down her arm through her fingers until she was surprised to see the water was fizzing. She shook her hand, rubbed her fingers, frowned, smiled doubtfully. What on earth..?

Beth rose to her feet, facing Tanya across the bed, taking her hand. The glass felt uncanny, as if it was glowing, though it wasn't. The despair and depression lifted in her mind. Maybe - maybe...

Tanya lifted the stone, Beth the glass. The girls reached out over the bed so that their fingers were touching both the glass and the stone. Beth concentrated fiercely. "Stone," she commanded it, "stone, make this water heal mum. For Christ's sake, amen." What else? Nothing. That was all she wanted.

She nodded. Tanya dipped the stone into the water.

94

Nothing happened.

Beth started to slump. She'd said it, she'd told Tanya...

The glass was growing warm in her hand. It seemed to be heavier, too, which was daft. But from somewhere a stir of hope, of confidence, came surging up in her, rising higher and higher. She had to clench her teeth to stop herself yelling in triumph.

"Yeah, the power's here. What now?" Tanya whispered.

"We give mum a sip," Beth declared. "Come on," she urged, as Tanya glanced at the 'Nothing by Mouth' notice. "Just a taste. If it's really magic, a sip's all it'll take."

Tanya let Beth have the stone, while she eased up the pillow with Mary's head on it, her mouth sagging open. Beth held the glass to Mary's mouth. The water flowed up, bulged at the edge of the glass. The marvellous strength inside her was trying to burst out. A tiny ripple trickled over onto Mary's slack lips, and Beth gasped with relief, release, as energy suddenly gushed out of her.

Behind them, the door opened. The nurse came in with two porters, saw what they were doing and shouted, "What are you at? Stop that! D'you want to choke her?" She dived forwards to seize the glass from Beth and glared at them furiously. "Never in all my born days - can't you read?"

They were paying her no heed. She turned to

tend to her patient.

Mary swallowed. Her lips were moving, sucking. She sighed deeply. Her eyes opened, blindly staring.

They all stood still. Mary sighed again, moved a hand, and then seemed to give up. She relaxed, settling back down into her lethargy.

"No! Mum, come back!" Beth leaned in close to her, shaking her hand slightly in her urgency. "Oh, mum, wake up!" she called. "Come on, mum, wake up! It's Beth! Tanya, help me! Mum, wake up! Oh, please, mum!"

Tanya reached out her hand and clasped Beth's, with the stone between their palms. They leaned over Mary, willing their love and care towards her, willing her better. "Come on, Aunt Mary!" "Mum, mum, wake up!"

Mary's half-open eyes slowly focused. She sighed again, and sniffed, her nose twitching comically. From blankness, her face turned to recognition, and a tiny smile. "...Beth..." Her voice was a breath. She licked her lips. "More, please... more..."

The news of Mary's miraculous recovery flew round the ward. Nurse after nurse, doctor after doctor stuck their heads round the door, delighted, congratulating her and the girls, taking her pulse, listening to her chest, examining her eyes and reflexes, until the staff nurse cleared them all out. "Let the poor woman have a bit of peace, now!" She went out last, smiling back at them.

Mary felt astonishingly well. Not full of energy, certainly, but alert and cheerful. Her face ached with smiling. Now she lay back, white and tired, treasuring her daughter's love and the glowing exultation in her niece's face as Beth held up the stone where her aunt could see it.

"Am I right?" she whispered. "It was the stone that did it?" She didn't believe it... but something had worked.

"Yeah, Aunt Mary. It were Beth done it!"

"Tanya made me." Beth was sniffing happily. "Both done a bit of it, I suppose, Aunt Mary."

"Thank-you both, then. I love you."

What was there to say, with Mary back from death's door? "Get yer anything, Aunt Mary? Some fruit? Shop's open downstairs, seen it on the way in."

"That's a kind thought." Mary considered for a moment. "Some orange squash, maybe? They'll keep me in for a day or two, I shouldn't wonder. You can dip the stone in it before you go, and magic it for me!"

"Sure thing!" Then Tanya's face fell. "Beth - you got any money? Never thought in the rush."

They all looked exasperated, until Beth's face cleared. "Mr Craig! He'll lend us some, just until we get back. There's all the people who left this morning - their money's in the sideboard drawer. We're not short, we just haven't got any cash with us."

"Completely useless, the whole lot of us!" Tanya left, chortling.

Behind her, Mary leaned back and eased her right arm, strapped across her chest. "Beth, how did you get on this morning? Did the breakfasts go okay? Was Mr Mandrake any bother?"

Beth hesitated. What should she say? All about Mr Mandrake's threats, and everybody leaving? She didn't want to worry her mother. But Mary, watching her, pursed her lips. "Look, love! I may not be well yet, but I'm not daft. If I think you're not telling me everything, I'll only worry. Come on, now! Spill the beans!"

Downstairs in the coffee bar, Mr Craig was overjoyed to hear of Mary's recovery, and absolutely refused to lend Tanya a couple of pounds. "It's not a loan, it's my pleasure, dear! My privilege! Oh, I couldn't be happier, really I couldn't! We'll get her some flowers as well. Come along!" He marched off to the shop. Tanya, slightly embarrassed, was towed along, her arms piled with roses, orange squash, a melon, grapes - "Green ones, of course, dear! Black grapes mean a funeral! Now, what choccies have you got, ladies?"

While he pondered over the small selection, two men in white coats joined the queue, laughing. "Parked right in the ambulance drive-in! He should lose his licence!"

The other agreed. "Anybody who can run that car doesn't need to worry about parking tickets. The insurance alone's probably more than my salary." He sighed enviously. "Wish I could afford it! Nothing like a Porsche to bring a gleam to a nurse's eye."

"But a gold convertible - a bit over the top, wouldn't you say, old boy?"

"Positively vulgar, my dear chap!" They laughed together.

A Porsche convertible. Gold.

The melon fell. "Oh, butter-fingers, Tanya dear - Tanya? Tanya!"

Luckily there was a lift just waiting. On Mary's floor, Tanya was first out, racing along the corridors and round the corners to crash into Room 4 and stop, panting, angry, her throat closing in fright.

Mr Mandrake turned towards her and smiled. "Hello, Tanya."

Chapter 8

Mr Mandrake was relaxed and totally at ease, perched on the side of Mary's bed. Beside him, Beth sat frozen by her mother's pillow, holding her mother's left hand far too tightly for comfort.

"Come in, come in! Ah, white roses. How unsuitable for your dear aunt here, and yet how suitable for me. The language of flowers," he explained, reaching to take the bunch from Tanya. He sniffed luxuriously. "Ahh. A charming Victorian idea. White roses mean 'I do not love you'. 'Non amo te, Sabidi.' 'I do not love thee, Doctor Fell, the reason why I cannot tell; but this alone I know full well, I do not -'"

"Stop showing off!" Tanya snarled, dumping her other burdens sullenly onto the bed. "I knows why, too right I does!" He only chuckled smugly.

"You obnoxious man!" Mary's temper was giving her strength. "All this nonsense about curses, just because you didn't get what you wanted - I couldn't believe anyone could be so egotistical, so petty and self-centred."

He stiffened. "Let me assure you, madam, that the curse is by no means nonsense. Nobody, but nobody, will stay in your guesthouse for more than one night from now on. Everyone will feel the chill, the fear -"

"Fear? You say you've filled my house with fear?"

"Indeed."

She could feel it herself, the aura of evil that had spread through the room the instant he came in. At last she began to believe the incredible story Beth had told her. But still she fought back. "You sound like an old Hammer horror film." His eyes flashed in annoyance. "And even if it was true, I'm delighted!"

"What?" He rose in angry astonishment.

She pushed herself up off her pillows to face him. Automatically, Beth caught the grapes and the bottle of squash before they fell off the bed, and turned to put them on the locker. Wincing with the pain of her arm, Mary smiled tightly. "There are more than sixty hotels and guesthouses in Nairn, Mr Mandrake. Until now, mine was just one among many. But now it's special! I'll have ghost-hunters and thrill-seekers queuing up at the door!"

Tanya's face lit up in cheeky glee. "Good on yer, Aunt Mary!"

"Let's call the nurse," Beth agreed, "and have you put out!"

Mr Mandrake raised an eyebrow. The temperature of the room suddenly fell about ten degrees. "You underestimate me. Do you think that you have seen all my powers? Oh, no. You suspected that I had caused your aunt's accident, Tanya. You were quite correct." His face and voice were charming, but they drew back from him as if he had the plague. "And though she has made a miraculous recovery from her relapse - with which, as it happens, I had nothing to do - she is still unwell. I can - influence, shall we say? - her future health."

Casually he picked up the bunch of roses on the bed by his hand, and slowly twisted the petals off, flower after flower. "Unless I get the stone, now, it will be a cold day in hell before you are well again, sweet lady. You feel tired now? That's nothing to what you will feel. Weariness too great to let you stand, sit up, hold a book to read, lift a hand to feed yourself." Crushed white petals floated like funereal confetti onto the bedcover. Dismayed by the creamy venom in his voice, the blue flash of his gaze, the drip and drift of the petals, Mary sank back. "And nothing will show up on the tests. Nothing at all. They'll call it ME or something, I expect. But you'll know. Won't you?" He laid the empty stems gently down on the dying petals.

Satisfied by their appalled silence that he had made his point, he relaxed, shrugged, smiled genially round. "But it doesn't have to happen. Just the opposite, in fact. You could recover incredibly fast. And I'll even throw in a sweetener. I don't honestly believe your joy at the spell on your home, so I'll go back and remove it. Return the house to its previous happy state. After I get the stone. There, now. Health and prosperity, in exchange for stone with a hole in it. A mere pebble. A more than fair offer, I'd say. Well?" A surge of force radiated from him, holding them still and afraid, pressing them all to agree, to submit, to surrender the stone...

Mary was scared. She couldn't believe it. But she had to... Inside, she quailed in terror. Stuck in a hospital bed, helpless, until she died... Oh, no! But she forced herself into frail defiance. "No, I'll not have it! Give you what you want, make you even stronger, encourage you to hurt more people to get your own way next time - no!"

Beth was too scared to speak up. Her mother was far braver than she was, opposing Mr Mandrake like that. She didn't want him to get the stone - but what could they do? Any of them? If he did what he threatened, mum would be a cripple... until she died... Oh, no!

Rigid beside the bed, Tanya felt as if she was going to burst with rage. Her ribs ached with the seething pressure of her fury, but she couldn't let it out - not here. He had described his powers before and although she hadn't believed it before, she did now, utterly, now that she knew what she felt inside herself. But she mustn't let it loose, not here in a hospital, not until she could really control it. She was helpless, held by her own power.

Mr Mandrake was quite confident. "You have no chance. One way or another, I'll have that stone. You can't get it away. Give it to me.

Now." His tone commanded instant obedience.

At last, Beth found her voice. "It's not - it's not true." She sounded hoarse. "If you were so confident, you'd not be making these threats to frighten us into giving it to you."

"Oh? Are you absolutely sure?"

No, she wasn't.

Sullenly, hating her defeat, she reached into her pocket and took out the stone. Mr Mandrake purred in satisfaction.

Beth looked at the stone for a long moment. She drew a deep breath - but could find no words to say what she felt. Her face bleak, her heart raging, she held out the stone.

Tanya reached out and took it from her hand.

Everyone looked at her as if a statue had come to life. For so long she had been quiet and still, they'd almost forgotten she was there. What would she do?

She didn't know. She felt like a volcano in the Antarctic; roaring hot inside, against the chill of this man and the cold of the stone in her hand. If she lost control and let her rage blast free at him, she might blast off the roof too.

She stared across the foot of the bed at Mr Mandrake. "You said as I had power. You willing to risk a curse?" Her tongue felt swollen and dry.

He chuckled, watching her carefully. There was something about her - an aura - careful, now... "My dear, your puny curses couldn't harm me. Against an unwary or unskilled person, yes. But don't try any tricks on me. The stone, if you please!" He held out his hand.

She ignored it. If she didn't release the pressure just a little bit, she'd explode. "You wanted me to work for yer. Okay. I'll scry for yer."

"Don't try to fool me, Tanya," he warned her. "It won't work."

She shook her head, grave and stern with the strain of holding herself in. "No trick. Just the truth." Raising the stone to her eye, quivering with tension, she looked through the stone straight at him. Her voice was stiff, distant and cold as a polar wind, and in spite of all his armour of power and confidence, the hair on the back of his neck prickled. "You thinks as yer all-powerful. But it'll come for yer, same's for anybody, in the end. Soon. I can see it. Can see yer, in the stone here. Lying dead in a grave at crossroads, wi' a stake through yer heart."

The chill in the room was broken by Mr Mandrake's sudden yell of laughter. "Oh, Tanya, Tanya! What a let-down! Who do you think you are - Peter Cushing? Oh, dear! Trying it on, my dear child! You've been watching too many Dracula films. Stakes through the heart, indeed! I am many things, Tanya, but a vampire is not one of them. I fear you'll have to do your homework better than that if you plan to scare me!"

The others looked embarrassed.

Tanya didn't move, except to lower the hand

holding the stone. She gazed at him, remote and untouched by his jeering. The pressure inside her was just about manageable now.

At length his laughter faded, and he held out his hand and snapped his fingers for the stone. Rather to his surprise, she laid it in his palm with no further argument. Sitting still on the bed, he weighed it in his hand. "So this is it. Kenneth Odhar's scrying stone. So small, and yet so powerful." He lifted it and looked through it. They tensed, but he shrugged and shook his head. "No. Apparently I need to work through a medium with it, as I do for dowsing. You wouldn't care to help, Beth? Ah, well." He stowed it in his breast pocket and stood up. "Goodbye, then, and thank you for a most interesting and profitable time. Straight down the A9, stop over in - York, perhaps, a delightful city - and I'll be home in London tomorrow."

"What about the spell?" Beth demanded. "You've to go back to Nairn first, to lift the spell off the house."

Mr Mandrake smiled across at her, that charming smile that didn't reach his eyes. "You really are far too credulous, Beth," he murmured. "Why should I bother? I already have what I wanted."

Mary gasped. Tanya seemed to swell in rage. "You rotten so and so!" She would have gone on, but Mr Mandrake lifted a hand and she froze.

"You will mind your tongue." The warlock's voice was venomous again. "I've had just about enough of you. You've given me so much trouble, you and your family here. And you struck me. I really can't let you get away with it, my dear. I believe I'll leave you with a little token of my regard. Blindness would be suitable, maybe. Or - no. You have a foolish tendency to speak out of turn, young lady. From now on, you'll be dumb! Dumb as your own stone!"

In a whisper, Mary screamed, "No! Stop it!"

Concentrating fiercely on Tanya, Mr Mandrake raised his right hand to point at her - and fell forwards across Mary's knees as the bottle of orange squash thudded against the back of his head.

Beth dropped the bottle on top of him, shuddering. "Is he dead? Have I killed him?"

Mandrake's body slipped slowly backwards off the bed, almost dragging down the drip-feed tube with him, and thumped onto the polished, vinyl floor. A few displaced white petals drifted onto his hair.

Gulping in shock, Tanya stiffly bent down to check. "Neh. Stunned, is all." She stood up unsteadily. "Ta, Beth." She took Beth in her arms, rocked and patted her for comfort. "'It's okay, Beth. Okay. Wow, that was a near one!"

After a moment, Beth managed to control herself, and gave a weak smile. "I'm okay." She looked down at the unconscious man at her feet. "Oh, dear!"

Mary took Beth's hand. It was trembling. So

was her own. She made herself stay calm. "Well done, Beth. You had to stop him. You did the right thing. I'm proud of you!" Oh, she was so tired! "But I don't know what we'll tell the police."

"Can't hang about for them, Aunt Mary."

Beth pulled herself together. "No. We've got to get rid of the stone."

"Then he'll go away, maybe, and not bother us any more," Mary said hopefully.

Tanya sniffed. "We should be so lucky!"

Beth shrugged. "Yes, I know. But even if he does, we must get rid of it."

"Where?" Mary demanded wearily. "Where, that he can't find it?"

Tanya knew. "In the quarry."

"The Lochloy quarry?" Mary asked.

"Yeah." Tanya nodded to them. "It come to me last night. Perfect. Iron, to stop the spells, see, an' -"

"Well, now, Mary, here you are at last! It's taken me absolutely ages to find you!" Mr Craig was talking even as the door opened. "How are you, dear? Tanya just waltzed off - Good gracious!" Chocolates in one hand and melon in the other, he stared at the polished shoes poking past the end of the bed. "Beth, dear - Mary - there's a man down there! What's wrong with him?" He set down his gifts, fussed round the bed and bent to look more closely. "Deary me, it's Mr Mandrake!" He looked round them all in astonishment. "It's Mr Mandrake!"

Mary's lips suddenly twitched. "Yes, we know."

"But - but what's he doing on the floor?"

"Lying on it." Tanya exchanged a faint smile with her aunt.

Mr Craig stared. "But - what happened? Look at these poor flowers! Did he slip?"

"Yeah." Tanya smiled, more definitely. "Slipped up bad."

He was shocked at her callousness. "I must get a nurse!"

Beth and Tanya grabbed his sleeves. "Hang on a tick!" "No, Mr Craig, please wait!"

Unwillingly, he paused. Mary reached out her good hand to him. "Mr Craig, you drove the children here, didn't you? Please, take them back again. Right away."

"Yes, of course, Mary dear, if that's what you want!" He sounded puzzled but agreeable. Beth and Tanya let him go. "I'll just get a nurse first." He had scurried out before they could stop him again.

"Oh, no!" Mary lay back, white as her own pillows. "Look, you've got to get the stone away from Mandrake. And the police. Somehow. Whatever else we do."

"Yeah," Tanya agreed. She was on her knees, rummaging in Mr Mandrake's pocket for the stone. "Got it!"

"But what about you, mum?"

Tanya stood up. "Ey, look, if we're away when he wakes, he'll chase us, an' not wait to cast any spells here. Right? Godzilla'll be a babe in arms compared to him. But I been knocked out, I know what it's like. He'll be shaky, see? So it's the best thing us can do. Draw him off, an' get rid o' the stone."

"But how?" Beth cried. "Mr Craig'll waffle on for ages -"

"Get a taxi," Tanya said calmly. "Bound to be some downstairs, delivering visitors."

Mary, fighting off a faint, forced herself to be encouraging. "Yes... Best chance, anyway. Go on, love! Beth!"

"Yeah! Move yerself!" Tanya hissed, grabbing her cousin and shoving her towards the door as a nurse came hurrying in. "Go on, down to the car. I'm right behind yer!"

Beth looked back at her mother. White and exhausted, Mary made herself nod, smile, gesture her daughter away. "Go on, Beth!" she whispered. "I'm fine!"

She didn't look fine, Tanya thought. And when the Mandrake man came round... But she had to go; Beth hadn't the sense to cross the road without her! The nurse was bent over Mr Mandrake, checking his pulse, Mr Craig fussing behind her. Tanya patted Mary's hand. "We'll cope, Aunt Mary!" she whispered, and ran, catching Beth just as a lift door opened.

Beth felt all wobbly as they hurried along the corridors to the exit. Tanya's arrival, the fight with her, Mr Mandrake, the dowsing, the accident, the responsibility of looking after the house, her mother's relapse, the magic of the stone, the threats, and finally, to top it all, her own breakdown into violence. She couldn't believe she'd done it. Hitting somebody on the head! Even if it was to save Tanya. She couldn't stop trembling.

Tanya shook her head as she helped Beth along. Shock. Conscience. Gentle, Beth was. "Ey, there's that Mandrake's car. Right in the road o' the ambulances, just like them doctors said!" She stared round. "Just our luck, not a taxi in sight! Oh, what do we do now?"

They gazed at each other in frustration for a moment. Then Tanya yelped. "Beth! Beth! Didn't yer say as you could drive a tractor?"

Beth gaped, scarcely understanding.

"Oh wake up, dozy! You can drive, right? So drive yer mam's car! A tractor ain't that different! Or I can try."

That woke Beth up. "You? No way! If anybody's going to drive mum's car, it'll be me!"

"Right! There it is. Come on, then!"

The car doors were locked.

"Oh, no! The keys! Mr Craig's got them!" Beth moaned.

The hatchback door swung open. "Yeah! Thought he might have forgotten this one." Tanya reached over the rear seats to unlock the doors.

"What's the good?" Beth protested. "We haven't got the keys!"

"Keys? Who needs keys?" Tanya pulled off one of her silver earrings, straightened out the wire loop, dived down under the dashboard and fiddled about with the wires there. "Gotcha! That should about do it. In neutral? Right, put yer foot on the gas a bit, Beth!"

Her jaw dropping, Beth pressed down on the accelerator. To her mixed dismay and delight the engine started.

Tanya struggled up from her crouch, grinning widely. "Right, let's get off before Mandrake wakes up. Oh - hang on a tick!" Leaping back out of the car, she picked something out of a waste bin and raced off towards the hospital again.

Beth bit her lip. Keep the rules - usually. This was an emergency, she knew that. But... She was scared stiff.

Tough.

She practised going through the gears until Tanya reappeared, grinning. "Stuck broken bottles under his wheels. Hold him up a bit, if he can't magic up a couple o' new tyres! Give us more time, eh? Right, I'm set!"

Beth looked round at her. "You realise this is illegal? And dangerous? I've never driven on the road, I've no licence, I'm underage and I'm not insured. Are you positive you want to risk it?" Tanya didn't bother answering. "Okay." She took a deep breath. "Fasten your seat belt. Here we go!"

By the time they jerked to a halt at the traffic lights at the hospital entrance, fifty yards away, Tanya was already clutching the seat. "Take it

112

easy!" she gasped. "Kangaroo petrol, is it?"

Beth wiped her forehead. She was sweating already. "Look, this wasn't my idea! You want to walk?"

Tanya opened her mouth to say yes; but the lights changed to green, and the jolt as the car started again clacked her teeth shut. She swallowed, and hung on.

Chapter 9

Slowly, with grim determination, Beth fought the car into submission down the road. It was not the same as a tractor, lighter on the wheel and far heavier on the brakes, and there was other traffic to terrify her. She didn't even notice the small first roundabout. Luckily nothing was coming at the second; she didn't manage to stop in time. At the third, she misjudged the speed of an oncoming lorry. Brakes and horn screeching, the driver swearing, white-faced, it swerved round her.

"Took ten year off me life, that did!" Tanya whispered.

"What?" Beth was too busy inching the car round onto the Nairn road to pay much attention.

"Oh, nothing." Don't distract the driver... They bumped off the pavement. "Look, d'yer want me to drive?"

Beth almost ran the car into an oncoming van as she turned to stare at Tanya. "Bad enough me driving it. Don't be daft!"

"Okay, okay! Watch the road!" In her turn, Tanya wiped her forehead.

Mr Craig had been frightening; this was pure terror. On every curve, either way, the big car swerved wide, out into the centre of the road; clipped the verge fifty yards later as Beth overcorrected... At least they had no problem about overtaking; the only things that didn't pass them were bikes. Beth nervously swung in towards the side whenever a car swept past.

After a while, relaxing a touch, she dared to go up to third gear, to a fairly steady thirty miles an hour. "This is fast enough."

"Yeah!" If anything, it was too fast. But Beth was doing her best. Tanya could have done better herself. About thirty miles an hour better. But it was Beth's mum's car.

Roadworks held them up, too. At one junction the road was a single lane alongside a deep ditch where drains were being laid. Beth nearly knocked a blue-tagged post into the ditch, but then stopped almost neatly in the queue at the traffic lights, a cautious twenty feet from the car in front, changed carefully into neutral, and with relief pulled on the handbrake. She sat back, easing her shoulders, rubbing her hands to dry them, quite pleased with herself. "So far so good! Halfway. Only about five miles now, into Nairn, and then another half mile on the other side. Here we go again." She gritted her teeth, crunched into first gear, and was moving cautiously forwards when suddenly she gasped. "I feel dizzy."

Tanya put a hand to the wheel, to steady it. Just in time. Beth suddenly screamed and jerked wildly. A traffic cone went flying. The tarmac edge crumbled under the front wheel...

"Ey up!" Tanya hauled at the steering wheel

and just managed to turn the car back from going over. Beth was holding her head, crying out in pain, kicking out, pressing raggedly on the accelerator. "Ey, stop it, Beth! What's wrong? Stop!"

Beth couldn't stop. The car, fortunately only in first gear, jerked and raced up to over twenty miles an hour as she thrust herself back in her seat, moaning, clutching her head and shaking it wildly.

They had been going so slowly that there was a long gap in front of them. It was just as well. Under Tanya's desperate hand, the big car was weaving unsteadily from side to side. At the end of the single lane, she managed to steer out onto the full-width road, past the staring faces in the cars waiting to pass the red light at their end. Stop now! Glad it wasn't an automatic, she banged the gear lever into neutral, steered to the side of the road, and hauled up the handbrake. The car engine was roaring. So what? It wasn't a bad place to halt, other cars could pass easily, but she wouldn't have cared if it had been in the middle of the rush hour. They were stopped. That was all that mattered.

Suddenly, as quickly as it had overcome her, Beth's fit was over. She relaxed, took her foot off the throttle. The engine's rage died gratefully to a throb.

Nearly as shaken as Beth, Tanya put an arm round her cousin's shoulders. "What were that, Beth? Him?" Beth nodded, staring in fright.

"He's woke up? He knows?"

"He's raging. He's coming after us." Beth had felt it, somehow, when Mr Mandrake recovered his senses. She knew what he was doing.

He had staggered to his feet, oddly alert but light-headed, sick, detached from his surroundings. One thing filled his mind; the stone. *His* stone. Those girls had stolen his stone. Again. Get it back. Now!

He was in a different room. Mary wasn't there. Furious, he transmitted a wide-ranging blast of rage. Everyone inside the hospital winced at the sudden jab of pain. Mary cried out, and the nurse bringing her some tea jumped and spilled it.

For the moment, though, he had lost much of his control. The frenzied outburst hurt him, too. He had no energy to spare. Nor time. He'd deal with Mary later. Now, he must hurry, catch those brats, get the stone. *Get the stone.* Then they'd see what he could do!

How long had he been unconscious? Ten minutes? Longer? Where were they? He was still faintly tuned to Beth's mind since he had helped her dowse. He felt carefully along that frail link... She was driving. They weren't near the quarry yet. His anger struck out at her, and in satisfaction he felt her scream and swerve.

Follow her. Get the stone. Some fools were trying to hold him back. He pushed past them towards the exit. He felt as if he was in a bubble. The world outside was clear, but at the same time distant and unimportant. He had to get the stone.

"Keep still, wait, have a cup of tea, lie down! Well, if you must go, you'll have to sign yourself out, we can't -" The staff nurse swung round, waving the unsigned form angrily. "We should have stopped him!"

At the front entrance, the porter was furious. "That your car? Get it shifted! Now!" Mr Mandrake didn't bother arguing; he was as keen to get it moved as this fool was. The engine started with its usual deep snarl. The tyres screeched.

"Hang on," Tanya was saying. "Better not be moving when he finds the glass, eh?"

Beth moaned in anticipation. "Oh, dear... Oh!" She sat up with a jerk. "It's blown. He's stopped... Agh!" She was rigid with the agony in her head. "I can't see!" Her vision was full of black and red whirling spirals of pain and tension.

"Hang in there!" Holding her tight, Tanya muttered in her ear. "Oh, what's he doing to yer? He's a monster!"

A thought came to her. She felt in her pocket for the stone, and held it against Beth's forehead. It was warm to her touch, and seemed almost to quiver... "Does that help at all?"

Beth's eyes opened painfully, and she nodded. "I can see. Don't let go, Tanya!"

"Should I drive?" Tanya asked.

"No!" Beth could even laugh a little. "No, I'll

manage, thanks. In just a minute."

Even though the nuts spun smoothly under the wrench, though the car rose steadily on the jack, changing the wheel still took time and attention. As Mr Mandrake turned to the practical details before him, the pressure on Beth eased. She sat up. "Let's go! I can drive. Yes, I can. I've got to!" She slammed the car into gear.

"Watch out, now!" Tanya cried.

"Okay. Okay! But he's not going to beat us! You'd better keep the stone handy," she said, trying to smile. "He'll be back. And Tanya, please, hold me. It's easier when you're touching me. Maybe you keep him off me, somehow."

Tanya moved as close to Beth as the seats would allow, to shelter her, strengthen her with her presence. She hugged Beth's shoulders and held the stone against her neck, ready to grab the wheel again if she had to.

Beth knew it when Mr Mandrake tightened the last nut. He didn't even stop to pick up his spare wheel. The stone was getting away! The wheels screamed on the road. Straight through a red light at the hospital entrance he whirled, and paid little more attention to the roundabouts than Beth had done.

"He's coming." Beth's voice was flat. "He's after us."

Tanya bit her lip, her hands itching to take the wheel. "Fifteen miles, just... He'll be up wi' us in no time. Can't yer go faster, Beth?"

"No." Beth's tone was quite definite. "Not if you want to get there in one piece."

Tanya turned to stare out of the back window. They were stuck behind a bus, just coming into Nairn; and the Porsche streaking after them...

Maybe it'd get caught at the traffic lights at the single-track section.

It didn't. A big gold car roared past.

All the time, Beth was fighting against a twisting surge in her mind. 'Stop!' it urged her. 'Swerve, there's a child in front of you! You're going too fast! There's a bike! Too fast!' Keep to the facts. Check speed - twenty-five. Not too fast. The bus slowed, stopped; she passed it. 'Swerve right!' No, keep straight. The road was clear, no dogs or children or bikes. Round the roundabout, carefully. Change up to third. Not far now. Road clear. Keep going, don't let him distort what you see, what you do. 'Slow down!' No. 'Dodge that cat!' No cat. Go on.

At last, there was the lane. She just stopped the car at the side of the road and they piled out. Down the track, over the gate, through the barbed-wire fence, amongst the bushes.

"Ey, were only the day before yesterday we was here! Seems like months!"

In the tiny clearing, Beth sank down onto the stones above the water's edge, exhausted, her hands shaking. "Well, I've done all I can. And he's right behind us. I can feel him, closer and closer."

Under the reflections of sky, leaves and their own faces, the rust of the old cars gleamed in the dark water. Tanya took Kenneth Odhar's stone out of her pocket. "Ain't much, to cause such a kerfuffle."

"Can we really just throw it away?" Beth asked. "Won't he just fish it out? Use his magic to - call it, somehow?"

Tanya puffed in exasperation. "Oh, no! The iron'll stop 'im. He ain't - what's the word? Omnipotent. Got his limits. An' he won't hurt us, neither. We'll see him off. You ain't got no squash bottle handy here, but you'll find something. An' I'll curse him!" Beth almost smiled. "We'll be okay. Listen!"

A powerful car roared up the road just beyond the bushes, and screeched to a halt.

Beth looked scared. "Go on, then! Throw it into the water!"

"Yeah." What else had they come to do? But the stone clung to her hand...

Mr Mandrake's voice, full of power, echoed in their heads more than in their ears. "Don't move! Stand still. Don't move a muscle!" He was already in the lane.

Beth was trembling. He was coming for them....

Borne up by sheer temper, Tanya flung herself into her habit of disobedience. She'd had a lot of practice fighting him recently. She lifted her hands and threw the stone with all her strength. She sagged with relief. It was gone! Or was it?

No, it was still in her hand. It had wanted to

be found; it didn't want to leave her.

The gate creaked under Mandrake's weight.

"Oh, no!" Beth was sobbing.

"Stand still!" The furious force of the warlock's command was so great that they stiffened, even Tanya. But his concentration wavered as he got caught in the barbed-wire. The fence squeaked and twanged. The bushes thrashed.

Suddenly, Beth reached over, took the stone from Tanya and tossed it into the quarry hole. There was a splash, small, insignificant, at the same moment that the warlock thrust into the little clearing.

He glared round. The girls stared back. He strode over to the edge of the pool, raging, "Stop! Come back! I command you! Rise!"

The water was disturbed by the reflected ripples, broken into tiny winks of grey, green, brown, blue...the red of the rusty cars, that stopped magic... It smoothed to ripples, to calm, and there was nothing but the dark water reflecting the trees and the sky.

Slowly, white with frustration, Mandrake turned on the girls.

Beth held Tanya's hand, to give and get support. She wanted to be sick, to turn and flee. But not while Tanya was there. She was needed. She couldn't leave Tanya to face him alone.

Tanya wanted to be sick, too. The anger she had felt in the hospital hadn't been able to vent itself, nor had time and calm to ease away. It was boiling up again inside her, stirred up by her fear, heaving, hurting, burning mentally and physically. She let it swell. In the hospital, she'd been afraid to let rip. But out here, she didn't care.

Beth, pale and shaking, was forcing herself to stay and protect her. A paper hankie against a hurricane.

Warmth for her older cousin, so gentle, kind and brave, flowered in Tanya, and she turned fiercely on the warlock, like a mouse facing a tiger, ready to fight for Beth as well as herself. Did he know she was so dangerous? Or was he in any state to care, if he did know?

She gritted her teeth. She'd make sure he found out, and if he didn't care, she'd make him!

Unless his power was really so much greater than hers that he could wipe her out...

No, that just wasn't true. It mustn't be true! Deep down, she knew, without ever letting the thought take shape, that her certainty and confidence were her only defence. If she didn't believe in it, absolutely, her power wouldn't work. She had to believe, for Beth's sake as well as her own. She did. She must. Of course she did.

Mr Mandrake regarded them for a moment, unspeaking. He didn't feel light and detached any longer. His head was pounding and he was having some difficulty focusing his eyes. The girls blended together into a single, dark figure, solid as rock, outlined in gold light against the green blur behind them, and then split apart again into just Beth and Tanya.

The stone was gone. He said it, to be certain, to stoke his anger. "The stone. Kenneth Odhar's scrying stone. It's gone."

"Yeah." Tanya tilted her head towards the pool. "In among ten ton o' iron. Yer can't get at it now."

His lips twisted in a soundless snarl. "But you're still here." His tone was heavy with menace.

Beth shuddered. To his astonishment, Tanya laughed.

"Something amuses you?"

"Yeah. You." Teeth clenched, she stepped forwards between him and Beth. "Yer can't do nowt. You touch us wi' yer magic an' whammo! I'll blow up in yer face." Scared, and more stubborn, defiant and aggressive because of her fear, she watched his certainty waver, and pressed on. He felt ill after the blow to his head; good! "It were you said us had power. Got more'n yer knows. Just busting out me skin this minute." She was smiling tightly, inching forwards towards him, feeling the confidence, the rage, the pressure of power rise in her. "Just try casting a spell on us. Go on. Try. Or touch us. Go on. Touch us." She held out her hand, almost eagerly.

Mandrake drew back. Round her the air was crackling with energy like static electricity. His arrogant superiority wavered. He wasn't at full strength now, while he was still shaken. There was no hurry. Leave them to think about it - yes, that would be best. Let them wonder when... Later, when he was fully recovered, he'd demolish her. Shred by shred!

He glared, frustrated by his unexpected doubt, and the thumping pain in his head. "You've thwarted me again, Tanya."

He was backing down! "Heh! Where's yer moustache to twirl?"

Sneering, he turned to the easier target. "You, Beth, you dared to strike me."

Beth was having trouble staying upright. "Yeah." Tanya spoke for her. "Belted yer a good one, didn't she? Real squash champion."

"I'm sorry," Beth whispered. "I didn't mean - I'm terribly sorry -"

"Ey up! Don't crawl, Beth!"

"A pity you stopped her, Tanya. I was enjoying it." His voice was again smooth and controlled. "Relax, you're quite safe. For now. But don't forget me, will you? Because I'll be back. Some time. And then -"

"And then what? Know what you are? Cruel." Her face showed her disgust. "You're such a bully. Thinks you've got the right to do what yer fancies, just 'cause you've got the power to."

"Of course! What else is power for?"

She frowned, struggling to say what she meant. "Got to be more to it than that. Helping, making things better, not worse!"

"How childish!" he sneered.

"As you grow older, my dear, you may want to use your power for all kinds of things - good and bad."

Tanya hesitated. "I doubt it. I want to help Beth and Aunt Mary." She faced him bravely.

He raised a hand to stop her. "You're quite safe, Tanya. And Beth. For the moment. But I'll go past the hospital on my way home. I shall call in to visit Mary again. Briefly." He paused to watch Beth's face crumple. "Paralysed, deaf, dumb, blind, in constant pain - I don't think your mother will enjoy her life from now on, Beth."

Tanya leapt at him, her hands raised, forgetting her power, her fear, everything in a mad longing to claw the sneer off that handsome face. He laughed and hit her; not with power, but simply with a punch on the chest that knocked her down to kneel, winded on the grass. He looked down at her in satisfaction. "Stay there, my dear. And say a prayer for your aunt. She'll need it!"

"Oh, mum!" Beth was sobbing. She slipped to her knees beside Tanya; she couldn't help it. "No, please!" she begged. "Oh, mum! No, please, don't do it..." But she knew he wouldn't stop, she couldn't stop him.

He waited for a few seconds, relishing her terror, and then as Tanya started to recover he turned away. In another minute the roar of the big car's engine faded up the road.

Chapter 10

Her face swollen and blotched with crying, Beth turned to Tanya. "Stop him, Tanya! He's going to cripple mum! Stop him, please!"

Tanya knelt quite still. Her head was splitting with pressure of rage. Her heart was thudding, shaking her, hurting her with the pounding. She drew a great, shuddering breath. In her mind, she formed the words: 'Curse him!' She whispered them; called them aloud. "Curse him!" But they were just words. "Can't do it. It don't mean nothing." Not yet...

The power was there, but she must deliberately pour it into her will. And that was a dreadful, terrifying thing to do. To kill someone - even him - knowingly.

She must be sure...

She turned to Beth. Beth's trembling suddenly stopped. She rubbed a hand over her face, smearing away the tears.

Tanya's face was solemn. "Beth?"

Beth was equally stern. She nodded, slowly. "Yes. You've got to. We've got to. We can't let him hurt mum. Please, Tanya. I'll help. Anything, anything at all, only stop him. Save mum."

Tanya sighed. This was the reason, the permission, the spur she needed. "Right, hold me hands."

Kneeling in the sunshine, they joined hands. A rush of force sparkled in every nerve of their bodies.

Beth carried their sight down a long tube, like a glass telescope. The image at the far end came rushing towards them. A great, golden car, racing along the road, well over the speed limit, but they were zooming in to poise close above it.

The driver was thinking about Beth, sending pulses of malice to increase her pain and worry for her mother. She winced, but the malevolence goaded her on, hardened her against him. His hair was blowing in the wind. He rubbed the back of his neck, shook his head as if he could feel their gaze, and looked round, but there was nothing there. They watched as he frowned, then laughed, tossing his head back in a vicious triumph and anticipation of Mary's destruction. The car bulleted forward.

Tanya concentrated, moulding the pressure of energy inside her chest, inside her mind. She started to mutter. "Curse him. Oh, curse him dead, before he can hurt Aunt Mary." No; blank out everything, except her target. Him. Nothing else in her mind. Just him. "Curse him. Mandrake. Curse him." This time, it meant something.

The car swept up a hill, flew over the crest. There, ahead, the warning signs for the roadworks at the crossroads. Single lane traffic - eight hundred yards, four hundred. Traffic lights. Green, about to change to red.

Mandrake reached out with his mind to hold the lights at green for his convenience.

"Curse him..." Tanya released a touch of the pressure.

He winced at the sudden surge of pain in his head. The lights turned red. Irritating. They must be put back. Only a few seconds, traffic at the other end of the lane wouldn't have started to move yet. He concentrated on the man working the lights. The man's hand moved to change the lights back.

"...now!" Tanya let loose all her fury and frustration, all her fear, all her loathing, all her protective love of her aunt, projecting a great thrust of raging power.

The warlock's sight blurred for five seconds. He was under attack! Who - Tanya! He struck back. Tanya screamed in agony. Mandrake's vision cleared sharply -

A tractor and trailer, moving out from a side road, blocked the road ahead.

Mandrake slammed on the powerful brakes. Plenty of time -

A shred of glass, tiny and unnoticed, tucked into the tread of the left front tyre, pierced through. The tyre exploded.

The car hurtled, screeching down the road, swinging from side to side as Mandrake fought to control it. Its front wing clipped the trailer, sending hay bales toppling. It was past, spinning helplessly now, skidding onto the single lane, the ruin of its front wheel sliding over the edge of the four-foot ditch. The bonnet dropped, plunged into the gravel bank on the far side. Engine howling like a wounded tiger, the car somersaulted high, tossing the driver out of the open top.

Tanya and Beth watched in cold determination as Mr Mandrake's body fell onto one of the surveying posts, dragged it from its place, and slowly, in a little avalanche of sand and pebbles, slid down the side of the ditch to crumple mercifully half-hidden in the shadows at the bottom; the blue plastic tag on the wooden post through his heart glinting falsely bright and cheerful red in the sunshine.

The girls sat back, collapsing onto the grass, silent, exhausted.

At last, Tanya raised her head from staring into the pool, to find Beth watching her. "Is that it, all past?"

Tanya nodded. "He's dead." She shuddered.

Beth hugged her awkwardly. "It wasn't for yourself, Tanya. It was for mum. And..."

"Yeah. Like yer said. Everything dies sometime. It's still..." She started to shake, sobbing tears in Beth's arms.

"I know. I know. It's all right, it's all right..."

Eventually, Beth pushed herself to her feet. "Come on. Home." As she helped Tanya up, she started to count. "You came on Tuesday. And - him. You found the stone yesterday, and mum was hurt. And today's just three days." She shook her head wearily. "I feel a hundred years older."

"Are a hundred years older. Twelve going on

a hundred an' twelve, that's us. We seen things as most people never imagines is real. An' done 'em, too. Makes a difference. Only natural."

"Natural?" Beth tried to make a face of exaggerated surprise.

"Ey, come on. Don't joke about it."

They stood up and moved towards the fence. Tanya turned to look back. Pity...

She stopped.

Where Beth had tossed the stone, something just under the surface was making a tiny flaw in the ripples.

While Beth watched her, she went back, knelt down and reached as far as she could. Yes, she could just reach it. Lying on top of an old car, just below the surface, waiting for her, calling her back to find it and give it a meaning again...the scrying stone.

She sat back, with it in her hand. With this, she could - she could channel her power. Get rid of the spell on the house. Make Aunt Beth happy and well again...anything.

Although it hurt, she held it out to Beth. "It's yours as much as mine."

"No way!" Beth drew back in alarm. "I don't ever want to touch it again."

"'S'okay. Not evil, not itself. Helped us wi' Aunt Mary, didn't it? An' we'll need it, to find the curse he left. Just a - a control. Like a machine yer turn on an' off."

But it had called her...

"Come on, Tanya. Home."

The car was still there, its near wheels run half up the grassy verge, the engine running quietly. Beth smiled a little. "I'd forgotten all about that."

Tanya nodded.

"Yes," Beth sighed. "Can you turn it off, Tanya?"

"The engine? Yeah, but -" Tanya blinked. "Ain't yer gonna drive us home, then?"

"No."

"Why not?"

"It isn't an emergency any more." At Tanya's stare, she shrugged. "Well, is it? We've broken enough rules for today, don't you think?"

Puffing in bewilderment, Tanya reached into the car and tugged the wires apart. Yeah, she supposed Beth was right. Get back to the real world. She ran to catch up with her cousin. Her blistered feet hurt. That was all right. She had to pay somehow...

After a while, Beth put her arm round her cousin's shoulders. Tanya stiffened, and then relaxed and slipped an arm round Beth's waist. In a companionable silence, supporting each other like Siamese twins, they walked home.

Chapter 11

On the threshold, the chill swept over them again. Shivering, gritting their teeth, they marched in. Mrs Craig wasn't about. "Where's she gone?"

"Out. Don't blame her none, neither. Feel like leavin' meself. But I ain't gonna let him beat us now!" Neither of them would be first to mention Mr Mandrake's name.

They looked at each other, sagging in depression. "Mum said it would be a tourist attraction," Beth ventured, trying to fight it off. "Haunted house, and so on."

"Neh." Tanya shook her head. "Don't believe it. No ghosts here. Just nasty an' cold an' hostile." She braced her shoulders. "Gotta do something about it!"

"What?"

Tanya reached into her pocket. "Could we - you know - use it?" In her fingers, the stone lay heavy and cold.

Beth's face showed her agitation. "How?" she demanded.

"Look, I knows just a bit about it," Tanya said. "From Cat, see? He must've made a charm, a real thing, like, as a focus for the curse, an' hid it someplace. To work when he weren't here, see? Get rid of it, an' that'll be it done wi'."

"Really? Really over, for good and all?" Beth

brightened instantly. "Can you find it with the stone?"

"Can try." Reluctantly, Tanya raised the stone to her eye and peered through. "Neh. It's no good. Just shows dark." Beth sighed. "But it might work as a dowsing pendulum. An' if I can't make it work, I think you can."

"Oh, no! I can't! Not again!"

"Okay." Calmly, Tanya accepted her cousin's distress. "If yer can't, yer can't. Don't blame yer, not after - an hour ago." She sat, turning the stone over and over in her fingers, and finally shrugged. "Give it a whirl. Come on, then."

Together they went up the stairs to Mr Mandrake's room. The bed where they had sat so excitedly to try dowsing for the first time stood stripped, its duvet and pillows dumped aside on one of the single beds. With a resigned grimace, Tanya took off her cross and slipped the chain through the hole in the stone. She held out the improvised pendulum. "Where's the charm, eh? Mandrake's curse. Where is it?"

She was disappointed when the tingle in her hand didn't come. She tried again and again, but finally shrugged. "Just have to look. Cupboards, loose boards an' that. We'll find it."

As before, it was perhaps the lack of pressure that encouraged Beth. "Silly, to be afraid of a pebble! And even mum didn't think dowsing was so bad." Biting her lip, she held out a hand. "I'll try."

She held the chain at first as if it had a

scorpion on the end. "What do I say? 'Where's the curse?' Will that do?"

"Why not?" Tanya shivered. "Get a move on, before we perish."

"Right." Beth braced herself. "Where is the curse? Is it in here?"

Nothing happened.

She tried again. Still nothing. "Maybe it was him made it move before?" she suggested hopefully.

"He said yer a scryer. Could be yer needs somebody else. An' he said we went together." Tanya laid her hand on Beth's arm. "Try now."

Beth jumped. The touch of Tanya's hand had given her a slight shock, like a brush from a faint electric current, scary but exciting. "Right. Where is the curse?"

"Look!"

The stone was starting to swing. Not in a circle. Swaying to and fro, between the door to the back stairs and the back wall of the room. Towards the door, the swing increased. It led them out onto the landing, into the small bathroom, and finally circled when Beth held it above the middle of the floor, about two feet from the side of the bath.

"Under here. Feel the chittering cold? Trying to drive us off."

"Yes. Under the floor? But -" Suddenly Beth's voice rose in discovery. "I know! The builders! They had the side of the bath off! Just a couple of screws each end. I'll get a screwdriver!" She paused on her way out. "You were right, what you saw in the stone. It will be all black in there!"

Two minutes later they lifted the bath panel aside. A gush of cold, foul air made them cough and choke, but a triumphant certainty pushed them on.

Tanya lay down to reach her skinny arm deep into a break in the floorboards below the bath, and started groping about. "Ey, what a stink o' mushrooms! Must be the dry rot. Oh, I'm all mucky, I wish this stuff'd dry up an' blow away..." She scrabbled about, her thin face smeared black. "Filthy in here, an' rubble, an' - can't get in much further... Ey, what's this? Yegh! It'd make yer sick!" She pushed herself up, holding the thing she had found as far away from herself as possible. "What is it?"

Screwing up her face in distaste, Beth peered at the horrid little bundle. "That's a seagull's claw. And a dead crab. And damp seaweed, and a bit of net. And a fancy stick, shoved through the net to hold it all together -"

"Ain't just a stick, it's a magic marker. See them leather thongs an' the bit of lead, an' the marks painted on it? It's a message, a kind o' control, like, tied to them things to tell 'em what to do. Them dead things an' the net an' that, he must've gone down to the shore an' hunted 'em up last night - ey, it were just last night! When I said the stone were gone. Cold an' wet an' stinkin' an' binding - that's what it means.

Just like them nightmares." She nodded in satisfaction. "This is it, all right."

"So what do we do with it? Put it in the bin?"

"Neh, get rid of it proper. Pull it apart an' burn it. That'll sort it."

They turned to put the side of the bath back on, and Beth suddenly clutched Tanya's arm. "Look!"

"What?" Tanya couldn't see anything.

"Look in the hole!"

Tanya peered in. "Don't see nowt - oh." The hole was dirty, certainly; but the black fungus had vanished. The wood was grey, old, but sound. The stink of mushrooms had gone.

"You did it, Tanya!" Beth whispered, her face breaking into a wide grin. "You remember? You said you hoped it'd go away. Dry up and blow away, you said. And it's gone!"

Tanya grinned. "Ey, steady job that, I could eradicate dry rot for a living!" They started to laugh, hysterically happy, collapsing over the bathroom floor.

At last, Beth sobered. "Come on - let's get rid of this curse as well!"

They made a small fire out in the garden, with newspaper and sticks, and laid the sickening little package on it. The flames almost died away under it. But as the wooden stick burned, the seaweed and shell and bones charred and shrivelled, blackened and fell away to ash, and the fire, the whole day, and their spirits, blazed up bright and high at last.

☠

Warm and comfortable again, the house was busy all weekend, with at least fourteen people for breakfast every day. The girls were kept busy, with no time nor energy to brood. Beth worried about the dark melancholy that showed when Tanya wasn't smiling. But with time and hard work to take her mind off it, she'd get over it.

Tanya was glad to see Beth recovering fast, back in her normal, bright world.

Mr and Mrs Craig left on Saturday. "See you again next year, dears - though really, after the way you behaved at Raigmore, but then we were all in a state about Mary, poor dear, weren't we? Miraculous, wasn't it? And dreadful, that accident, just terrible? But what could he expect, with a big, powerful car like that, and the state he was in? Give our love to Mary, dears, I always say -"

"Harold!"

"Yes, dear, coming!"

The girls waved them off cheerfully. Tanya was grinning. "Ey, isn't it quiet?" They laughed together.

Mary came home on Monday, hobbling, bandaged and slung, constantly smiling in delight as they boasted of how well they'd coped. She sobered when they finally got round to talking about Mr Mandrake. "I can't be sorry," she said, settling into her big armchair with a mug of tea, her bad ankle up on a stool. "It was unbelievably horrible. And such a tremendous relief, though I shouldn't say so, when you phoned to say what had happened."

She patted Tanya's hand. "Try to - I can't say forget it, because you won't. Never." The child looked quite hollow, somehow. "But you acted to help somebody else, not yourself. That makes a big difference."

Beth nodded. "Same as I had to hit him, right, mum?"

Mary snorted. "We were lucky there. I said he'd slipped, and when he woke up he was in such a hurry to get out that he didn't explain, or we could have been in real trouble."

"Real trouble? Compared to him?" Beth looked incredulous.

"An' I didn't just thump him, Aunt Mary." Tanya's tone was flat, her eyes dark.

"I know, pet." Mary shook her head. "Well, I don't know. It's so incredible. Oh, I know you believe your curse worked. But did it?"

"What?" Tanya's eyes lifted to her aunt's face in surprise.

"Maybe the accident would have happened anyway. And you just - saw it, somehow, without actually causing it."

Tanya sighed, rather disappointed. Aunt Mary was trying to help, but had slid into the old, patronising, adult-to-child style. Kids don't, can't, mustn't do anything seriously important. Tone it down, make it ordinary. Pass anything mystic off as imagination, forget it, it didn't really happen.

But that was muddled thinking. Tanya knew what she knew.

So did Beth, exchanging a long look with her.

So did Mary. But she didn't know what else to say... She smiled at them. "At least you can relax now, Tanya. It's all over."

Tanya shrugged. "Ain't all over, Aunt Mary. Not for me." She crossed to the window and stood looking out.

Beth wasn't surprised. "You mean, you're going on? You'll use your power again? I won't. Never. You keep the stone. I'm scared of it."

"Huh!" Tanya snorted. "Think I ain't?" She took it from her pocket, to stand holding it, cold and heavy in her hand. Just a stone - until it was touched with power... She turned round, dark against the light behind her. "But I got it. An' I got this power. An' so I gotta learn how to control it, 'cause it won't go away." She smiled at Mary's astonishment. "I'm scared. Ain't fun, real magic."

Beth wanted to be properly sympathetic.

Tanya's lips twitched. Typical Beth. "Yeah, Aunt Mary, it's true. Don't know what I'll do -"

"You'll stay with us, of course! You'll stay, my dear, as long as you want to. You're family, Tanya. After what you did for me." Mary frowned. "Oh, come here, pet!" She held out her good arm.

Tanya came over to her chair, to sit awkwardly on the arm and be hugged by both of them. But she returned to her main point.

"Can't stay for ever, Aunt Mary. Got to get Cat to put us onto somebody as can teach us proper. Not like - him." She laughed again, rather wistfully. "Used to want to be a witch. Kid's stuff. Now I knows I can, it ain't that easy. Cursing works both ways. Yer pays for what yer does. Every time."

Beth nodded. She knew.

Mary sighed with relief. As long as the child knew that, there was hope for her.

"Can't go through life like that, not thinking o' nothing but yerself all the time. Pure waste. Gotta be a use for this, not just for me, but for everybody. I gotta learn how to control it, so's if I slip on a stair an' say, 'Oh, hellfire!' the whole place don't go up in flames."

She sniffed as Mary and Beth laughed.

Beth nodded again. She pitied Tanya. "Twelve going on a hundred and twelve," she murmured.

Her mother's eyes rose quickly to her face, and returned to Tanya's. "Remember, love, you've got us, family. You're not alone." Must get her back to real life... "But right now, we've got a whole pile of laundry to finish. Come on, get a move on! Switch on the iron and magic some of those pillowcases flat for me!"

Tanya laughed, stuffed the scrying stone into her pocket, and turned with relief to ordinary things.

For the meantime...